THEN WE SAW THE FLAMES

DANIEL A. HOYT

THEN WE
SAW THE FLAMES

STORIES

UNIVERSITY OF MASSACHUSETTS PRESS

Amherst

LC 2009010038
ISBN 978-1-55849-699-6

Designed by Kristina Kachele Design, llc
Set in Chaparral with Priori Sans display
by Karen Mazur
Printed and bound by The Maple Vail Book Manufacturing Group

Library of Congress Cataloging-in-Publication Data
Hoyt, Daniel A.
Then we saw the flames : stories / Daniel A. Hoyt.
p. cm.
ISBN 978-1-55849-699-6 (pbk. : alk. paper)
I. Title.
PS3608.O9575T48 2009
813'.6—dc22
2009010038

British Library Cataloguing in Publication data are available.

For Sarah, who reads all the pages.

CONTENTS

THEN WE SAW THE FLAMES

LAST CALL OF THE PASSENGER PIGEON

DARREN FELT HIS BOOTS being embraced by the mud. He felt the wind crinkle his ears. He felt the old man's finger poking into his arm, into his skin, bone, muscle, fat—there were so many layers in a human being—and then the old man made a tight shrill cry, nothing like a man. He did it again and again: *keck, keck, keck.*

"That one's been dead for fifty years, sixty years," the old man said. "The bird's extinct, and the call's extinct. Nearly extinct. I'm the only one keeping it alive."

Darren wanted to be anywhere, even school, except out there, in the swamp the old man called an ecotone. Ecotone—it sounded like a brand of guitar. The bugs squished into Darren's ears and his eyes and his nose. His mother made him do it. He did just about anything she said, and in return, she let him do whatever he wanted, and she never noticed when the whiskey bottle had drained itself of another half-inch. So he was there, smelling the wet mudstink and sitting in the itch of green. The old man made Darren's face break out. The old man was the opposite of Clearasil. The old man wanted to teach Darren all of these fucking, old, tweety-bird calls.

A clump of milky black-mottled bird shit splashed to the ground between them, and Darren said, "It's an omen."

"Don't be a burden on my patience," the old man said.

The old man's white skin had lapsed into brown, like a mealy apple, peeled and then discarded. He had a fringe of dandelion fluff for hair, and one of his eyes was red-veined and smoky—it hurt to look at him sometimes.

The old man made two long *ka-pweeets* followed by a series of *chilks*. The *chilks* made Darren's hair bristle up along the back of his neck and way up inside his ears.

Chilk, chilk, chilk.

"If that's a mating call, I don't see any women running over, no birds neither," Darren said.

The old man's mouth made a slapping sound.

"Burden on my patience, burden on my fine disposition," the old man said. "I'm keeping these calls alive. These birds live through me, and you can't even pay a little bit of attention."

"I said I'd come. I didn't say I'd pay attention," Darren said. "I don't give two shits about birds."

The *chilks* started up again. The old man's lips were puckered into a liverish O. The pink seemed to have bled out of them. He sucked the capital O down until it became lowercase, and the *chilks* became deeper and quicker.

Darren tried to watch the old man's lips and picture Laurie's lips at the same time. He tried to picture Laurie's breasts and the line where the swimsuit had cut a boundary between the white of her ass and the brown of her tanned legs. That line was important. He got to cross it, with his eyes, with his fingers. He pictured the redheaded woman who worked with his mother. She took her clothes off for money. That's what they did there.

As if he cared about that. As if he cared, as if he cared. His words seemed lost. He was thinking in whistles. He watched the old man's lips, and he made his own fizzling noises that sounded more like bugs than birds.

The swamp had bushes and tall spindly trees like the spokes of a fence. Everything was trapped by that fence. Everything was too alive, fraught with green. Everything smelled like something was dying.

The night before, Darren had sketched the Aerosmith symbol, the one with the wings, on the back of his hand with a black Bic. He wanted to look at it, to see if it was too smudged or if he could resurrect it with more ink, but instead he watched those old lips. They were the brown of summer grass.

"I have all my own teeth," the old man said. "That's important. Take care of your teeth. Don't let the dentist pull any of 'em."

By the end of the session—the old man called them sessions—Darren could make the proper first syllable of the *ka-pweeet*.

"Passable," the old man said. "But you might never have the lips for the *chilks*."

Darren felt strangely insulted.

The old man drove, dropped Darren off at home.

"Place needs some paint," the old man said.

The house, more of a camp really, looked like a sunburned shoulder, red and peeling. Darren didn't say anything. The house didn't really belong to them. He cracked the car door, then waited a minute. He was supposed to get paid for this bullshit.

"Tell your mother I said hello," the old man said, and then he counted six dollars out into the flesh of Darren's palm.

Darren clicked out of the car without a word, kicked through the dust of the yard. Inside the house, his mother sat on the floor in front of the couch, right in front of the box fan. She was on the phone.

"I know. I know," she said, and she said it too loud because of the whiny churn of the fan.

She was younger than all of the other mothers he knew, and sometimes she called Darren "little brother." She was wearing a long white T-shirt that said "Orange Crush" in blue lettering, and almost the whole length of her brown legs stuck out from underneath. Her legs looked funny somehow, and Darren didn't want to look at them. He looked at the words "Orange Crush," but that's where her tits were. Someone had once said about his mother, "She has ass up to her tits." He forgot who said it. He looked at her hair instead. It looked like Farrah Fawcett's.

"I know, I know, I know," she said into the phone, and then she mouthed the words "hot dogs" to Darren. In the kitchen, he picked one of the hot dogs out of the frying pan with his fingers. He took a sip from the open beer on the counter and chewed the hot dog into oblivion.

"I know, I know," his mother said in the other room. She sure knew a lot of things. She sure was loud about it.

"Who you talking to?" Darren yelled.

"No one," she yelled back.

He drank another swig of the beer and ate another squirmy hot dog right out of the pan.

"You drinkin' my beer?" his mother said. She was in the kitchen now. She pulled her hair back into a ponytail, and then she let it go. "Wash your hands," she said.

"That old guy's kind of fucked up," Darren said.

"Don't say that," she said.

"He's kind of weird."

"We're lucky to know him," she said. She held the beer can up against her wrist and then drank for a long time from the can.

"You workin' tonight?" he asked.

She nodded and got another beer out of the refrigerator.

"I'll have one, too," he said.

"You will not."

Neither one of them sat down at the card table. Darren washed his hands and then ate another cold hot dog. This time he speared it with a fork.

"Manners," she said.

Darren smoked a cigarette and waited for Laurie out behind the high school.

Way past 10:30, and maybe she wasn't coming. He tried to snuff out the thought along with his cigarette butt. It was dark, and a patch of sweat glued his T-shirt to his back. She wasn't coming. Fuck. Shit. No. Yes. He could see Laurie now, walking toward him in the chalky dark of the night.

"Hey," he said, and she said, "Hey yourself," and then she pressed up against him, and she pressed up against him, and she pressed up against him, and they were rolling in the grass. They only pulled their jean shorts down as far as it took. If you took off all your clothes, you'd itch all night. There were bugs in the grass, some kind of chemicals, too—they had found that out already. They didn't say anything, and she was biting his bottom lip, and his hands were on her ass. She was holding his hips, and he was holding her hips, and he was touching her neck, and his hands were up under her shirt, and his hands were back on her ass. He wished he had more skin, more hands, more fingers, more of her, and then she twisted her hips a little to the side, and he felt himself turn into Jell-O, into gasoline, into a liquid that ran down the grassy hill and far away from him and tried to reach the sea. It would never reach the sea.

"You like that?" she asked, and she was a little out of breath.

"What do you think?" Darren asked.

They both pulled up their pants, but they lolled there, still touching, and Darren could feel the pulse of her running up through her breast and into his hand. She was seventeen, and she had a gap between her front teeth, and she wore Black Sabbath T-shirts and paisley bandannas. When she wasn't wearing headbands, she feathered her hair. He had watched her do this once. It took forty-six minutes.

"Did you get those Skynyrd tickets?" she asked.

"Not yet," he said, and they breathed in more of the dark.

"I had to go out with that old guy again," he said.

"The creepy one?"

Darren said, "He, like, teaches me to make these sounds in the woods."

"Fucked up," she said.

"He says that he knows all these birdcalls, for living birds, for extinct birds, and he wants to teach someone all of them before he dies or some shit."

"Double fucked up," she said. And then they were kissing again.

Darren made three bucks every morning for cleaning up the bar. Some mornings it was worth it, and some mornings—when someone had puked all over the men's room—it wasn't. His mother got him the job. The bar was long and cramped, really just two trailers shoved end to end and covered with mint-green stucco. Inside, there was a long Formica bar, and there were four tables and one platform where women danced and took off their clothes, except for their underpants. The bar was called Satin, and men drove up from Naples and Fort Myers to go there; that's what his mother said. Sometimes she came home drunk, and sometimes she came home when her pupils were the size of Peanut M&M's, and sometimes she didn't come home at all.

"All I do is tend bar," she'd say. "That's it."

Darren pretended that he didn't know what he actually knew.

No one had puked, and no one had pissed on the floor, so it was a good morning to clean.

He snuck a little bit of liquor, just a swig, out of the three open bottles behind the bar. He collected six cans of beer, two half-crushed. One had a cigarette butt rattling around inside it. He poured the juice from all of them, except for the one with the cigarette butt, into a paper cup. As he drank it down, he thought about lips—the old man's, Laurie's, his own, the red lips of a girl who hated him. Who knew whose lips had touched this beer? People's tongues had touched it, too, and he slurped it all down in thick gulps until he felt a fizz in his brain, and then he smoked a cigarette.

He had a nice burn of pleasure in his skull.

It was summer, so he worked cleaning the bar, and he worked for the caterer, and he smoked cigarettes, and he fucked Laurie behind the high school. He felt the warm happy prickliness in his head. That's what he did. That's who he was, and he pressed down harder on the mop. He would scrub the smell right out of this place, but when he was finally done, it still stank—of cigarettes and axle grease, like some broken machine burning itself out.

He listened to Lynyrd Skynyrd until the music stopped mid-song. When he opened the hatch and pulled out the tape, the ribbon of the cassette blossomed into a black flower of knots and snarls. He would have to steal another copy, slide it down into his underwear in the last aisle of the Sam Goody.

Barb was the girl who hated him; she worked for the caterer, too.

They were scrubbing pots and pans and dishes, and Darren sloshed the water so it splashed up on both of them.

"Will you fucking stop that?" Barb said. It wasn't really a question.

"It's just water," he said.

She didn't say anything.

"Maybe some soap," he said.

Barb was allowed to work with the customers. Darren was supposed to just help clean up. Barb wore Izod shirts and sometimes even plaid skirts. She had plucked out all of her eyebrows and drawn them back on with something, maybe a Magic Marker, and she made Darren's jeans feel dirty even when he knew they were perfectly clean. Barb always wore makeup, and sometimes she changed her long white catering apron two or three times in a single day. She was seventeen, like Laurie, but she seemed even older. Darren would be seventeen in three months, but Barb would always seem older. She would always hate him. She had nice legs.

Darren dunked a platter into the water.

"Your epidermis is showing," he said.

"Good one," she said. Her voice dripped suds.

"How does Ed mess up so many pans?" Darren asked. There was no answer to this, and they just kept on scrubbing and rinsing and drying.

The caterer's office was really just a kitchen with three ovens and a big sink and too many pots and pans. Ed was almost never there. He just left his trail of dirty pans, spilled flour, potato peelings, and Darren tried to make the trail disappear. Sometimes he felt like he was cleaning up evidence. Darren made two bucks an hour under the table; Darren knew that Barb made at least two-fifty.

"I hear you're fucking Laurie McKinley," Barb said.

She said it in a way that should have bothered him but didn't.

"Well, I hear you're fucking Ed," Darren said.

"I'm not fucking anybody," Barb said.

She was so proud of it that it had to be true.

He looked at her lips, today a frosty pink.

"You know how to whistle?" he asked.

"Just shut up," she said.

That night Laurie never showed up, or she had already come and gone home before Darren got there. He waited for forty-five minutes, and then he rubbed his closed eyes until he saw fleas of light. He felt a bruise of pressure inside his face. He didn't want to cry. He didn't want to cry.

He smoked a cigarette.

He walked home and smoked two more cigarettes. Laurie this and Laurie that. Maybe she was fucking somebody else? If he were fucking Barb, he wouldn't have to worry about her fucking anyone else, except of course Barb wouldn't fuck him either. He'd never get to touch Barb's breasts, over or under her T-shirt, either way. Barb didn't have a slutty gap between her teeth. He didn't want to think about Barb. He didn't want to think about Laurie. In the morning he had to go back to the woods with the old man. He didn't want to think about that either.

His mother was gone. No note.

He drank two beers as fast as he could, hid the crushed cans in the trash bag, pissed out a waterfall—it looked just like the beer. All that drinking and it just came out like nothing at all. He tried to make the *ka-pweeet* sound, but it embarrassed him. He dialed Laurie's number but hung up before the phone rang. He thought about Barb's big fat breasts, which were actually neither big nor fat. They were medium skinny breasts, but that didn't sound right, not at all. Where the fuck was Laurie?

The blades of the box fan whirled around and pushed air at him. He couldn't gulp it fast enough. He fell asleep on the couch.

The old man had flaps of translucent flesh on his neck; they climbed up his cheek. Some were pinpricks. Some were the size of a pencil eraser. Darren wanted to reach over and squeeze one.

"Pay attention," the old man said.

They were practicing making the sound of a catbird.

You made it with the back part of your tongue and your throat. Darren could feel the vibration of it humming in his head, his voice box.

"Not bad," the old man said. "Not bad. Not good, but not bad."

The old man had brought a stick of salami, and he sawed off hunks of it with a Swiss Army knife. They ate it on Ritz crackers. The meat was freckled with fat and what looked like spots of blood. It tasted like someone's leg, the underside of a knee, and peppercorns and garlic. Darren liked the idea of this taste more than the taste itself, but they ate until only the red casing, almost plastic, and some of the crackers remained.

When the old man smiled, chewed-up crackers mortared his teeth. The old man covered his mouth, sucked on his teeth. The old man didn't bathe often or seem to care much for soap.

"You see that," he said, and pointed to a tree and the viny plant wrapped around it. "The plant's called a strangle fig. Birds love those figs. The birds eat the figs and then shit out the seeds, and in this way, things keep going on, except sometimes the figs kill the tree. On some level, all of life requires shit: bird shit, people shit, metaphorical shit."

"Shitty shit?" Darren said.

"You're not supposed to say shit. You're here to do some learning," the old man said. "I acquired your services from your mother. There are some that would abuse this, yank down your pants. There are sorts like that everywhere. But I'm going to teach you something. I'm going to teach you how to be a singer; you'll be one of the last. There's one up in Maine, can't do the passenger pigeon. The woman up in Nome, her calls are too shrill. Idaho fellow died last year."

"Why me?" Darren asked.

The old man said, "I ask myself that question, too."

Darren hid under the bush, squatted really, and he could feel the mud sucking away at his boots. If you weren't big enough, this place would swallow you up. He touched the moist earth with a single finger, scraped at it, held his nose with the other hand. He held his nose and blew through his closed mouth and felt his ears pop, and then he began to meow like a cat. He felt the delicate rumble in his voice box. He did this for several moments, and then they appeared: the catbirds.

Three of them—all slate gray—danced around him in the breeze, then they found roosts, and they meowed back.

They didn't trust him, they wouldn't come any closer than four feet, but they'd mewl at him, and he'd mewl back, and they were pretty in a wild skittish way. They were birds imitating cats, or some such shit, and he was a man imitating a bird imitating a cat.

Wasn't he a man? He had summoned them from the sky.

He didn't want to cry, but he wanted Laurie to.

"Let's sit up on the pavement," he said.

"The bugs," Laurie said.

He tried to make his voice low and mellow, but the squeak of a door kept hinging in.

He lit two cigarettes and gave her one. They sat across from each other, Indian-style. He could see her face squinched up behind the glow of the cigarette.

"Where the fuck were you?"

"Where were you?" she said.

"Where were you?" he said back.

Laurie was crying. He could tell by the way her breath snagged on something as it pressed out of her lungs.

"I waited for you," she said. "I was here, and you didn't come, and I got scared, and I left."

"I was here, too," he yelled. "I waited for an hour."

"You were late," she said. "I know you were late."

She was right. She had to be right.

They sat for a while before they started kissing.

When they finally got going, he was on top, and he could feel his knees grinding into the dirt and the pebbles, the rocks and maybe chips of glass on the pavement, and everything cut into the flesh of him. Everything cut, and everything cut. It felt too good to stop.

His knees hurt, and they were both out of breath. The night smelled like sweat and swamp gas.

"We live right near the beach," he said, "but we don't go to the beach."

"We're swamp people," she said.

"Ecotone people," he said.

"What?"

He said, "Tourists go to the beach."

He walked Laurie home but not all the way to her house. He wasn't wanted there.

The night didn't seem to hold any stars at all, almost as if they had been shaken out of the sky. They would have come down like salt and pepper.

On the way home, he stopped at the all-night grocery store. He bought macaroni and cheese and hamburger meat and Kool-Aid. He walked home with his dinner along the two-lane highway.

The old man sat on his red plastic milk crate, and Darren looked at him; Darren could have blown him away with a fart.

"Hold on while I smoke my cigarette," Darren said.

The old man said, "Burden on my time. Burden on my patience. Now hurry up and listen."

Darren tried to climb into the sound, but his mind took him elsewhere: to Laurie sprawled nakedly before him, to the soft cavity of Barb's neck where he could look down into the nook formed by her breasts. He imagined various shapes and sizes of nipples as the old man cooed and sputtered.

For two hours, the old man made strange clattering bird noises, and then he looked at Darren, said in his dry-wood voice, "You'll probably never make more than the simplest of calls, noises really, a mewling puss, a pollywanta, a tomcat yelp.

"I learned how to do this in 1925, and Old Sparzek, the one who taught me, was about 102. It took us months, and I learned them all: the passenger pigeon, the dodo even."

Darren pictured the old man with a much older man, a gathering of wrinkles, except of course maybe the old man, Darren's old man, was younger then.

"How come we can't do this at your house or something?" Darren asked.

"It doesn't sound right in a house."

Darren looked out at the scrubby pines and the ferns. Was it hotter out there in the swamp or did it just feel hotter because of the muck and greenery and the sun glaring down at you like you were a stupid piece of shit?

"It's like a sauna," Darren said.

"It's not like a sauna," the old man said. "Florida's a teakettle. Smell it. We're steeping in the tea of it."

"You're soaking in it," Darren said. "Palmolive. You know—like those commercials?"

The old man just squinted at him.

Three red candles and two green ones perched on top of the cake.

"It's like poker chips," the red-haired woman said. "The red ones are worth ten, and the green ones are worth one."

Then they sang, "Happy Birthday, dear Val, happy birthday to you," except Darren didn't sing at all.

The party was at Satin, and his mother was already laughing too loud.

All these people were there, men mainly, some local drunks, the red-headed woman who took off her clothes except for her underpants. The men were muscled and fat and wore tank tops or gray business suits. They were fiftyish. The old man was there, too, and he didn't belong there. He belonged out in the woods with his stupid whistles.

"I want a drink," Darren said to the red-haired woman. She was tending bar, and Darren stared down into the freckled cleft between her breasts.

"Isn't that cute," the red-haired woman said.

She gave him a cold can of beer.

"Don't let your mom see," she said.

"Is this really a party for my mom?" Darren asked. Across the room, his mother stood in a circle of men. She seemed to be dancing without moving at all.

"It's always a party, cutie. For everybody."

Darren drank his beer, and then he drank another. The redheaded woman lost interest in him, and no one ate any cake, and his mother danced without moving in the middle of her flock of men. She was drunk or something.

She hugged one of the men, and then she hugged another one, and then the old man said something, and everyone laughed, and then the old man reached over and grabbed his mother's breast, and his mother just smiled, laughed even. Everybody laughed. Darren saw it from the other side of the room.

He was late. Barb was already working.

"Ed's pissed," she said.

"Fuck Ed," he said. "How come Ed never helps us clean up?"

"Ed's the chef," Barb said.

"Fuck Ed," he said again.

They were supposed to clean up the VFW hall. The banquet had been grazed and abandoned. There were fingerprints in a slab of slickly iced cake; crumbs had ascended; the white tablecloths were blurred with red stains. Ed had served barbecued chicken halves, and the paper plates were littered with the remains of fowl: bones and bitten flesh, crispy shreds of skin, useless wings.

"Put the fucking chickens in this trash bag," Darren said.

"What are you talking about?" Barb asked.

"Just fucking do it," he yelled.

Barb's eyes jumped up in her forehead, and her lips went slack; they looked greasy all of a sudden, as if she had eaten all of that chicken.

"Fucking do it," he yelled. He stood right up close to her, too close for anything but kissing.

"Not the plates or the other shit," he said. "Just the chickens."

He could see a half-moon of dampness forming around Barb's right armpit. Her eyes looked bruised. She plucked each piece of bone and flesh with a thumb and an index finger. She didn't look at him.

"Here, chicky, chicky," Darren said.

Ed would fire him tomorrow or the next day or the day after.

He didn't care. He made her pick up every single scrap, and then she handed him the trash bag. It must have weighed twenty or thirty pounds.

He said, "You don't even have nice tits."

As he walked away, Barb made a sound like crumpling paper.

He carried his trash bag of carcasses back out into the night, through the path, along the two-lane highway. The old man's Cadillac was still in the parking lot at Satin. The windows were open. Darren spread out his chicken carcasses, across the seats, on the hood, the trunk, the roof. It smelled like dead matches and grease and the sickly sweetness of barbecue sauce that looked almost like blood. It didn't smell like chicken anymore. He admired all those little bones and all those little wings and all of that crispy flesh. It was a plague, a pestilence, an entire species burnt up and devoured and dead.

He told Laurie about his mother, about the old man, about the chickens.

"That's disgusting," Laurie said.

"He deserves it," Darren said.

"It's just a breast."

"It's not just a breast," he said. "It's not just a hand. It's his hand. Her breast. His hand."

They were smoking cigarettes behind the high school.

"He'll know it was you," she said.

"Could be anyone," he said. "Could be Colonel Sanders."

"I need to get going," she said.

He didn't say, "But we haven't even messed around," even though he wanted to.

He said, "I'm getting those Skynyrd tickets. Tomorrow."

She puffed on her cigarette. She was wearing one of her bandannas, but he couldn't tell what color it was in the dark.

"I'm walking home by myself," she said.

He tried to grab her hand, but she was up on her feet and gone. He spread out on the grass. He let his cigarette burn down to a nub. He whisper-sang, "That's the way uh-huh, uh-huh, I like it." He waited for the bugs to come tear up his flesh.

He slept on the couch in front of the box fan. It was too loud with the fan, too hot without it. He didn't really sleep at all. His mother wasn't home, and then in the morning she banged through the door.

"Levon's here to pick you up," she said.

"Who's Levon?" Darren asked.

"You know who Levon is." The words snapped out of her mouth.

The old man said nothing as Darren climbed in the car. The Cadillac still smelled like barbecue, and Darren could see greasy smears on the seats. As they drove, Darren imagined his own blood spattered out in the swamp, his headless body floating in the Gulf, bobbing on a wave. And I'm not even a beach person, he thought. Seagulls would dance and caw and pluck out his belly button. He felt a cold tickle of excitement in his guts.

Back in the swamp, the old man said, "I'm pretending last night never happened."

The old man belonged in some museum, locked up inside it, where he could make his mouth-fart birdcalls.

"Today," the old man said, "we're going to work on the passenger pigeon. We talked about it before."

Then the old man made the screaming sound, the long, high *keck, keck, keck.*

"How am I supposed to know that's what it really sounded like?" Darren asked.

"I'm telling you what it sounded like, and then I'm putting the sound in your ear. Even you will hear the truth that's blowing in your head."

"You know how to make a sound like a chicken?" Darren asked.

The old man was quicker than his age should have allowed. Darren saw the hand and then he felt the sting on his face and then he heard the slapping sound. It was like lightning—you had to wait a beat for the thunder, and when he heard it, Darren threw his fist out in a rough, graceless arc, and his knuckles met nose, lip, teeth. The old man tottered for several seconds before gaining a half-steady balance on spread feet.

Darren threw all of his weight into another punch, his fist met the flat rough side of the old man's head, making a dull hollow-melon thump, and the scrag of a body before him buckled then collapsed. On Darren's right hand, the index-finger knuckle had burst open on impact. The old man was motionless, face-down, his nose pressed into the dirt.

Darren said, "Come on. Get up."

He pushed the old man's body with the toe of his boot.

The old man knelt in the mud. He was bloodied and weeping. His nose was plastered sideways into his cheekbone.

Darren said, "Where does it hurt? What can I do?"

The old man snuffed and wiped at his face with his hands.

The old man said, "You want these things to die. They will die. They will die with me. They will rot in my skull."

Darren bent over to help the old man, and then he felt a flash of something cold and then hot and then painful right near his belly button. The old man's Swiss Army knife dripped with barbecue sauce, then Darren saw the barbecue sauce leaking through his T-shirt, down his shorts, down his leg.

The sky was filled with lurid sunlight, and the old man wobbled, walked, then ran into the piney woods.

"They're dying," the old man called, but Darren couldn't see him. The swamp was bloody with sunlight. The trees stabbed the earth. All the birds were dead.

"What's dying?" Darren yelled.

Oh, his stomach hurt, and Darren felt sorrow rasping through his lungs, up his throat, out across his clenched teeth. He started to make the noise: *keck, keck, keck.* He did it again and again and again.

Darren imagined panthers tracking the man along his trail of thin old-man blood. They would chew up his cartilage, crack his bones between their teeth. Darren imagined the old man's horrible *chilking* death. He would scream like some long-dead bird, a phoenix.

Darren made the *keck* sound, but the old man wouldn't answer back.

Darren could feel the liquid draining from him. It didn't hurt that much, unless he looked at it. He didn't want to cry.

He pressed his fingers into his balled-up T-shirt, which was pressed into his wound. He could hear the blood—it was laughing at him—and he pushed harder against the wound as he walked and jogged and then walked because the jogging made his stomach hurt even more. The old man had taken the car keys. Darren walked all the way to the grocery store, where the manager said, "Jay-sis mother of Christ," and called an ambulance.

"How'd this happen?" the doctor asked.

"Fell on a bottle," Darren said.

The doctor looked at him.

"And I hadn't even drunk all of the beer," Darren said.

The doctor had a yellowy-gray mustache, and he looked at Darren, his face, for several seconds. Time and the doctor's face pulled taut.

"I'm going to choose to believe this," the doctor said.

First came the prick of the Novocain—the hot sting of a beetle.

"Can you feel this?" the doctor asked, and Darren felt nothing.

He couldn't feel anything until after the wound was washed and disinfected. Then, he felt something peculiar—the tug on his flesh as the doctor sewed up the skin.

That wound will pucker into a pink smile of a scar that will last all through his days, and thirty years later, he will remember that strange deadened pull on his stomach as the stitches went in.

He's forty-six, and the doctors have put the stents—three of them—into his arteries. Darren's brain flames with unconsciousness, and still he thinks of it: That sensation offered a shiny-pink pull of comfort, of being dragged into some new place, some new shape.

He has not thought of any of these things, the Florida past, for years and years. That crazy old man used to take him out to the swamp. Darren used to be able to make bird sounds: He could whistle and call and make birds flit around him. Hadn't he been able to do that?

Val sits in the waiting room with Debbie and Trevor. Darren has to be okay. She says this to herself as if it's a prayer.

Life is too good not to pray in some godless way. Sure, Cleveland is cold and snowy and gray, like the entire sky is reinforced concrete, but she likes working at the doctors' office. Who would have ever pictured her, plain old Val, working with doctors, keeping their messy lives in order, lining up their appointments, turning the scrawl of learned hands into something actually readable?

Sometimes she drives past the sketchy bars near the airport and thinks about all of the bad girls inside—and the bad boys, too, the men who take off their wedding rings but never notice the pale stripes of flesh marking their ring fingers. There are so many different kinds of bad, and most of them aren't really bad, not really, not fully anyway.

She remembers that horrible old man who died in the woods. Even he wasn't so bad. He died of a stroke. Everyone knew it. The police knew it, but it still seemed like a good idea to get out of Florida, to move up to her sister's, up in Cleveland.

Darren was just about to turn seventeen.

Now Darren's a middle-aged man.

How did that happen? How does anything happen?

Darren never gets mad at her, even though she fucked up all the things that could've been fucked up when he was a kid. They never even talk about Florida, don't have to. The past is the past is the past.

Darren's kind to her. He's kind to Debbie. He's kind to Trevor. He's kind to the postman. And as they rolled him away on the gurney to the operating room, he said "thank you" to the orderly. She could hear him. She listens to him, and she listens closely. Once in a while, say as he putters around in the backyard with Trevor, when he rakes the lawn, there are these moments when Darren whistles, suddenly and inexplicably, almost like a bird. He's too busy. He's lost in the world. But Val listens, and sometimes, the birds of Ohio answer back. They call to him, and he doesn't even hear.

AMAR

YESTERDAY AMAR ATE half a box of raisins, two crusts of bread cemented together with toasted cheese, seven grapes, and three squares broken off of a chocolate bar.

He didn't have time to be hungry. Benji required the hours of the moon, and the restaurant demanded the hours of the sun, and the skinheads, their hate as dark as an eclipse, stole ticks of the clock from both celestial objects.

The skinheads were rude, beer-smelling, shaven but unwashed and pimply, and they wanted to grind his business under them, under feet shod with boots and cruelty. They took up the brain cells that Amar had reserved for other things: the dew of his (now absent) wife's morning kisses, how Benji had metamorphosed from babying to crawling to toddlering to talking, the pleasure of leaving Istanbul behind. Instead, the skinheads demanded this space, etched their thick black swastikas into the flesh of his memories.

Amar arrived at the restaurant, and Serge, who could lift kegs of beer with either hand and preached to Amar the need for swift and bloody retribution, was already at work, scrubbing the last limb of a swastika off the bricks with fierce effort and a metal rasp. Serge muttered something about eyeballs on skewers, and Amar watched silently as the graffiti surrendered the last of its obscenity. Serge, with wrists as thick as his ankles and coarse black eyebrows that made children instinctively burst into tears, was the only employee left, and Amar knew even Serge would wear away under the friction of hate.

Serge said, "We are Turks. Our fathers were warriors."

Silent Amar turned the sign to "Open" from "Closed, Please Come Again," which the skinheads apparently translated each night as "Please Defile My Restaurant." Silent Amar, whose warrior father had battled only him. Whose father had broken three of Amar's bones, including one for luck. Just thirty minutes after that last break (the ulna that time), his father won the equivalent of twenty-eight thousand German marks in a crooked dogfight and then disappeared for nine years. When his father came back, Amar, whose left arm shook perpetually, as if he were forever ridding his fingers of the dishwater's brine, made himself disappear, too, into Dresden, which now threatened to swallow him whole.

Yesterday Amar ate a wrinkled tomato, the too-moist half of a peanut butter and jelly sandwich, four figs that had been squashed to the bottom of the tin by the weight of their brothers, and twelve peppermint candies.

On the way to the restaurant, he walked past the punks with their cigarette arms and their cocaine nostrils, past the skins with their kicking legs and their holocaust mouths. Dresden, ruined and rebuilt and glistening in parts and broken still in others, even now, more than fifty years after the bombings. Dresden, his adopted home for eight years, offered places for all these fucked-up people, and he was sick of its hospitality.

Dresden, parts of it with a new veneer of cobble and mortar, except everyone knew about the cracks underneath and, more important, about how the stones had not been sturdy enough before. Dresden, with its streets snaking through his veins, from the days when he pushed the lunch cart, which had become the restaurant, which threatened to become a bankruptcy of empty bricks. Dresden, and Amar never even went to the church, which the Germans refused to refurbish, where the angels still kept their broken faces, but he knew all about it. After Amar put Benji to bed, those angels wrinkled up their concrete half-noses at him as if they were about to whisper. Amar wondered whether his ears or their rubbled tongues never allowed them to speak.

Serge, with his arms like legs and his legs like torsos, was already at work with the rasp and the tongue: "It would not hurt to slice one of them up a bit. The rest of them would hear about it, and in that way, they would feel the knife too."

Silent Amar wrote "Help Wanted" onto a brown paper bag with a coal-black Magic Marker. The skinheads left their mark each night and their urine scent, and somehow they did more than this, flavoring Amar's pizzas and kabobs with their fatal spices, manureweed or shitroot or killingberry, as if the customers could sense this colorless, odorless fictional taint. If they served two hundred lunches, he could pay the grocer. Three hundred and the butcher got paid too. Three-fifty and the rent was secured along with crisp new corduroy pants for Benji. Four hundred put some marks in Amar's pocket. Five hundred meant he was dreaming. For the last six weeks, they had served an average of 176 lunches a day.

Everything is fine, he wanted to say, finer than fine. He wanted to chant this in the street because the customers knew something was wrong, and he needed to do something right, and the police wrote the same reports in the same way with the same results: nothing.

When one of the skins came into the shop, Amar felt the hummingbird in his ribs trying to fly its way out. The skinhead's vomit-brown pants were ripped from knee to foot, he smelled of kerosene, and he had tiny beads of dark blue in the piss-yellow whites of his eyes.

He leered at Amar and said, "I would like to apply for this job. I am very good at making garbage, the kind you put on a plate and call food."

Silent Amar was not one of these savages. He shielded himself with courtesy, wrung the dirty wetness from a rag into the sink, and said calmly, "Will you please get the fuck out of my shop? Thank you. Thank you for getting the fuck out of here."

Yesterday Amar ate the glutinous remains of the chocolate-chip ice cream, the carrot sticks Benji would not swallow, and three corn dogs, the first of which was mouth-burning, the middle one tepid, the last as cold as February.

Serge worked the rasp but not the tongue, and even the tool had slowed down to a whisper. Silent Amar and Silent Serge made pizzas and kabob sandwiches and pencil marks that added up later to 157 lunches.

When the girl came in at three o'clock, Amar raised his hand for number 158, but when he looked at her, the pencil stalled. He tensed his right arm and its extra gristle of muscle, the only compensation for the wreck on the other side. The girl's purple hair had been swept into a storm of cowlicks, and Amar counted at least seven places where metal rings pierced the flesh of her face: lips twice, nose twice, eyebrow twice, cheek just once. She stood straight before him, not hunched, not weighed down by the misshapen hump of her back that she covered but did not seem to hide with her coarse gray linen shirt. She must have been eighteen or nineteen, maybe just nipping into her twenties.

"Sir," she said, the words dropping like oil in search of vinegar, "I'd like to apply for the job."

As the girl filled out the application form, Serge rasped in his ear: "It's a trick. She's one of them. Can't you see? She has a bomb strapped to her back. She smells like hate. She looks like disaster."

Silent Amar looked at the mound of extra flesh, not the girl. A back that broken could not be cruel, could not explode into shrapnel. When she was done, he looked at the form without looking at it.

He said, "You start tomorrow, Sylvia, 8 a.m."

Serge made the scalding noise of steam, but Amar, his groin flushed with blood, did not allow his ears to listen.

Yesterday Amar ate a plate of spaghetti buried under a frost of Parmesan cheese, a crust of bread, two eggs that had been boiled until their shells burst, and the pulpy juice of a fruit cocktail, which he slurped from the aluminum can.

Serge, his arms tied with knots of straining blue veins, worked the rasp so slowly it appeared to Amar as if the restaurant, and not the tool, were moving. Silent Amar blotted the white tile floor with the sting of bleach, cut onions until he was dry of tears, and stole watery glances out the front windows. His eyes skipped over the midnight punks shrinking in daylight and the old men in synthetic ball caps, and finally, at five minutes to eight, Sylvia pushed open the door.

All day long Amar taught her (and watched): how to fix the meat so it jumped onto the skewers (how the cords of tendon made her fingers dance), how to make the skin of the pizza bubble up like a blessing (how the heat speckled her tan eyes with black), how to stopper one's ears against Serge's complaints (how her shoulders surrendered normalcy as they became a back, which became a lump, which became a mystery).

Yesterday Amar ate three clumps of broccoli, the larger wing of a lop-sided turkey, three slices of bologna, and a bag of Fritos Benji had crushed into cornmeal.

No Serge at all, and Amar, his left arm supplying more pain than effort, worked the rasp to grind the graffitied slur out of the day. Amar's hands knew what to do: mop the morning grime away, pick the tomatoes that were fat with juice, cut pita into calm triangles.

He saw that Sylvia had a way with crust, so it came out of the oven light and crisp and brown on the bottom, unless the customer wanted it burned, and then she knew when the pizza was just on the right side of ashes. She wore the same linen shirt from the day before and the day before that, but even with his face almost buried in that purple hair, Amar could get no sense of her scent. She worked, and he worked, and he liked it, and she scrubbed the long black counter with care and effort, without a drop of griping or a sigh of perspiration.

At the end of the day, the ticks of the pencil added up to 223 customers, and Amar smiled at the gleaming white-tiled floor, the bare brick walls that looked a little stronger than they had the day before. They didn't need Serge to prop them up.

Yesterday Amar ate an éclair Benji had drained of cream, two pancakes toughened by the griddle and softened by syrup, half of a grapefruit seeded with sugar, and a dollop of blueberry yogurt on the eve of its expiration date.

Yesterday Amar ate seventeen peanuts, a confetti of iceberg lettuce tossed with purple cabbage, four slices of chicken congealed in yellow gravy, and three oranges wrenched out of their peels.

After lunch, 263 ticks of the pencil, Silent Amar opened his mouth and let things come out, things about Benji: his wispy black hair and his soft unwrinkled walnut skin and his sixty-seven-word vocabulary. How Benji's laugh turned into a peppermint smile. How Benji spent his days at Mrs. Steiner's while Amar worked. How at night Amar took Benji home and made him dinner and cleaned his corduroys and played imaginary games with a child's rules, flexible and fantastic, as if every event would turn out OK as long as Benji had a little more time to think.

Yesterday Amar ate two waffles steeped in chocolate sauce, five stalks of celery, the hard edge of a wheel of cheddar, and three biscuits that had become brittle with age.

Yesterday Amar ate three-quarters of a honey-graham granola bar, eleven french fries sodden with ketchup, two quarters of a mandarin orange, and a banana Benji had abandoned to bruises.

All kinds of customers—old women in cold-war babushkas, snot-fingered punks, young couples with delicate vegetarian wishes, even skinheads with downturned eyes and money to spend—seemed drawn to Sylvia. Amar thought of this and counted 313 strokes of his pencil.

Yesterday Amar ate a piece of chocolate cake stripped of its shell of icing, three half-nibbled hot dogs, a plate of yams mashed by a tiny fork, the touch of Sylvia's hand on his wrist, and innumerable kernels of corn sliced from the cob.

Yesterday Amar ate two blueberry bars, the core of an apple, seven potato puffs, a can of green beans left to simmer too long, the meat picked out of nine chestnuts, and a cupcake fringed with purple icing.

Yesterday Amar ate six beets stewed in their own broth, seventeen cashews, two wings from a scrawny fried chicken, and the unequal half of a Reese's peanut butter cup.

First he went down alone, and he and the rasp scraped away the swastika mess from the night before. Then he went back to Mrs. Steiner's, and he took Benji's muffiny hand in his, and together they walked a slow, crooked line down to the restaurant. Amar wearing worn leather shoes resurrected with polish; Benji scrubbed and rinsed and re-scrubbed because Sylvia wanted to meet him.

"I had heard so much about you," she said, "that I expected you to be bigger."

Benji hid his face behind cracks of fingers.

The work of pizzas and kabobs chased Sylvia and Amar behind the counter, and it drove Benji into the realm of strangers. Amar watched as they flitted fingers through his hair and tickled his strong, fat belly and made him fold his hand into gentle waves when they said good-bye. One eye on pizzas and one eye on Benji and one eye on Sylvia, except

Amar did not have enough eyes for this. At the end of it all, Benji, sitting on the counter, shook his bottle of root beer and took long fizzy sips, and Amar counted 373 marks made with the nub of his pencil.

"Amar," Sylvia called from the storage room, and for a minute, the softness of her voice made him think she could not mean him.

He parted the canvas curtain, and she stood in a halo of fluorescence. The room, crowded with half-gallon cans of stewed tomatoes, was so small that he stood under the light too, almost stole it from her.

She looked at him as she started to pull the jewelry out of her nose and her lips. The seven rings clinked one by one into his hand as if they were a debt paid with coins. He peered into the holes she had made in her own flesh. She showed him her teeth, and he wrapped his arms around her. The hump of her back seemed alive under her linen shirt. It fluttered with delicate muscularity.

She said, "Do you feel them, the wings?"

He said, "What?"

"The wings. I bind them up."

The blood left his pants for his face, and he felt too hot to be trapped under this light.

He turned, and she said, "Wait," but he didn't spin back to her. He split the dingy curtain open with his body.

One of the skinheads, all dusty gray eyes and shit-black tattoos, held a blushing-red apple out to Benji. No thoughts, just steps. In two steps, Amar had the apple in one hand and Benji's wrist in the other, his son's arm all bird bones and skin, no fat, no protection.

"Get out, get out, get out, get out."

He said, "You get out, too, Sylvia. Get out. Don't come back. Just get out. Get out."

He folded his son in his arms, and he tucked his sight behind eyelids. Fuck her with her purple witch hair and her angel talk. It was a trick, a cruel distraction. They were going to kidnap his son, carve him up, spit him out.

When all else fails, you can go home, Amar thought, so he did, dragging Benji halfway and carrying him the rest. He cooked macaroni and cheese with those little sausages for Benji, Amar's silent mouth cheating his son out of every fourth bite.

Benji said, "I make you a tiger," and Amar, though too tired to be a tiger, let him draw thin lines of night across his face with the ticklish felt of a Magic Marker.

They had killed thousands and thousands of Germans in Dresden, and it wasn't enough. They couldn't have killed eight more? Just the grandparents of the gray-eyed punk and the grandparents of Sylvia? Just one more bomb flipping out of an Allied plane, a Rorschach of blood, and Amar's present would have been preserved by the past.

Instead, the future cursed at him, and Amar tightened his belt to its last notch, put his son to bed. He had his son, and he had nothing else, except maybe, way back in the closet, he still had the old stolen pistol. Amar's father had said to him, "When they treat you like something the rats shouldn't even touch with their whiskers, the best thing, the only thing, is to have a way to kill them."

Perhaps, Amar thought, in this way and with that speech, the pistol had been given from father to son and so on, a redundancy of potential violence, since the time of Amar's great-grandfather, but when it came to Amar, it was no longer a gift. His father had become a croaking bundle of thorns in a bag of leather, and Amar had taken the pistol, three identical tan shirts, a ruined arm, one pair of checkered pants, the equivalent of ninety-three marks, and a pair of boots mended with copper wire, and he had climbed up into an airplane for the first time and pierced the sky and left only the past for his father. Way back then, he didn't think this would be the future.

Amar covered the pistol's threat with the sheen of a garbage bag and went across the hall. He would ask Mrs. Steiner, all iron skin and insomnia, to please come over. *Mrs. Steiner, will you look after Benji? I have to go kill someone. I won't be gone long.* Then he said it, omitting only the middle sentence.

The night welcomed him. Everything dark, except a fingernail clipping of moon. Amar knew these streets from the days of the lunch cart. He could hunt in them. He would start at the restaurant, maybe lie in wait.

As he walked through the cobbled streets, Amar saw nothing except his father's voice, black and thick and smelling of diseased teeth. His father's curdled voice saying, "Despise the things that starve you." A sentence to surrender to. Amar lifted his arms, and a whiff of his own rotting turnip flesh hit his nose. Then the pistol seemed to fly from father to son to son to son to the dumpster behind Amar's store, as if stopping the path of heredity required just a flick of the wrist and the Germanic urge to keep the streets clean.

Cleanliness. Amar wanted this too, and he drifted into his restaurant to scrub the day out of it. The skinheads had not yet left their mark on the bricks, and Amar needed some similarly unblemished space in his head. He had black Magic Marker lines drawn onto his face by his son, and he didn't care. This was the best kind of nihilism.

It was a luxurious lie to think she was an angel instead of some fucked-up Dresden girl with a heroin brain and a perforated face and a mound of pulsating flesh where her back should have ended. So much was just a fucked-up mass of impossible fantasies: revenge-soaked dreams and angelic sex, magical futures and heavenly something or other.

The real was the crowd right outside his restaurant: three raccoon-faced punks trimmed in black, seven-elevenths of a grass-stained football team, an old man tottering on drunken legs. This scrum of clumsy humanity pressed whiskey-dyed noses against his lighted windows and looked in at him. It took him a moment to realize they thought he was going to open for business.

He would, he decided. He would feed all the empty-bellied drunks wandering through the Dresden night. First, though, they could wait for him, and he cut thick slices of lamb right into the palm of his hand. When he raised the meaty fist to his mouth, sustenance tasted like defiance. Dresden felt paved with sympathetic wounds.

MARIA

NIGHT HAUNTS the sacred forest, but to believe this, one must view it head-on.

I never liked watching from the wings of the stage. You could see the pulleys and winches that made the curtains slip up and then crash down. You could see the backs of the chorus members' tunics where the stitches remained raw. You could see the (real) wood hammered up to support the (fake) trees. I liked it when Maria secured a ticket, when I had a seat in the house, when the sacred forest came alive before me like a dream.

On stage, Maria performed Bellini's *Norma* ninety times. I watched fifty-seven of those performances. That, of course, was long ago, and now only the phonograph and imagination allow me to hear/see the real Maria (the fake Norma) plead for peace, for war, for her secret children's death, for her secret children's life.

I didn't tell lies the way convention (and the journalist) expected me to. I served up the truth, albeit in judicious portions.

I told him about the (real) soldier. I served him the tapeworm (also real). I delivered the baby (mostly real).

Let me prepare the dish. It's meat served raw. It's dangerous, you say? Yes, some people see danger in a plate of raw beef. That's the way of the world, wobbly and cautious. Beef carpaccio was Maria's favorite meal. I kept my knives sharp, and I always interrogated the butchers. Butchers, like journalists, are the kind of men who look at you politely, but when you turn your back, they plan to drain the juice from your thighs. Butchers are the kind of men who don't mind a little blood. I suspect if I possessed the proper dangling parts and the capacity to grow a mustache, to grow bald, to wear trousers, I would have been an excellent butcher. I would trim the fat, and my knives would keep a keen, happy edge.

For twenty-seven years, I was her maid, and I saw her stripped to her panties, and I saw her wrapped up in silk, and I brought her tea at 4 a.m., and I saw her lost to laryngitis. Despite this, I was a maid only in the strictest sense. Sometimes I accompanied as she stretched her vocal cords. My fingers plinked away at the keys. I administered 3 a.m. doses of the talking cure. I counseled her in the ways of the planets and the curtsies and the forks and the napkins and the sky.

No one comes to see me except those who bring the food and those who take away the scraps. The butcher brings me the freshest meats. He has a rib-eye face, marbled eyes. He stutters, but he's kind to prickly old women like me. He brings me the choicest morsels that once dripped with recent life.

I cook all my meat until it wears a dress of ash. Then it is safe.

Once a week, the stuttering butcher joins me. He sits down at my table, he carves the meat, I offer up the prayer, and we eat a meal without words. We don't talk. We don't care. We chew.

This journalist wore a crisp dark suit, a white shirt, a black tie, and I told him, "Despite the appearance of my body, this is not a funeral."

He may have relinquished a smile. His face was shaped like an iron. It flattened all of his reactions.

At times, he pretended to know more than possible, and at other times, he pretended to know less. What a luxury it is to play that game.

He made several attempts to be ingratiating, and once he even attempted flirtation. He offered me the support of his arm. I did not tell him that age had inoculated me against all human charms.

Maria told me the story three times, and I simply told it once.

Maria and her mother and her sister lived in Athens then, and Athens belonged to the Fascists, not the Greeks. Maria was so young and so fat and so hungry, and the soldiers pounded on the door. They wanted to hear her sing.

She sang every word the Fascists wanted to hear.

One Italian soldier had a squat brown face like a spoiled pumpkin, but he had mottled green eyes like bits of polished granite. She fancied him, and he made a show of being courteous, of teaching her Italian.

This man came back night after night to hear her sing, and one evening Maria went for a walk with him. They walked and walked. Their tongues were exhausted from speaking. Maria's toes throbbed in her mended shoes. They found a field, and in this field, they found a haystack. One can lose things in such structures.

The soldier never again knocked on Maria's door.

One day after the haystack, a fortuitous delivery arrived at Maria's home: a three-pound bag of flour, fourteen candles, five pounds of sugar, ten pounds of salted beef. Maria was meticulous when recounting this list, and I enumerated it with equal care.

The journalist wrote every item down. I saw him underline the word *sugar*. It made his lips curl up.

Why did she tell me this story? She must have had a reason. I look for reason in all things. Our words must be reasonable. Our sounds must have meaning, or we might as well bang steel cans together and call it peace.

Our stories are currency. And she gave that story to me, and in the same way, I pass it on to you. Remember her. Pretend she was generous. Pretend she gave that story to you.

The tapeworm ran up and down and through her. It was ninety-seven centimeters long. This creature needed length. It stretched out, and it spiraled through her intestines.

This worm was a grayish pink, and it had delicate little hairs. After its removal, it continued to squirm, even with its head cut off. Maria thought this worm owned all her sins, ate up all her fats, swallowed her greed, devoured her lies, sucked up her infidelities.

The removal required surgery. Blood became involved. Maria's intestines were ripped open and then zipped shut. She was a tough woman. When they were done, she asked for a cigarette, and she puffed smoke out of her nostrils, and she asked me, "Did you see it?"

This journalist, he asked the same exact thing.

"I did," I said. "It was alive in a way you couldn't have imagined, and after it came out, even with the head sliced from the body, it spiraled and spiraled in that milky gray operating room. Everyone watched. It had a fury. It did not tire."

Maria had seemed quite charmed by this answer.

The journalist looked at me through his blurry eyes. He did not write this part down.

Night haunts the sacred forest, and when the worm came out, it was bereft of life, but nevertheless an orderly throttled it, tied it in knots. He threw the worm in a large steel trash basin and covered it with a bloody towel.

When the baby came out, it didn't move at all. It was deposited in a similar basin but with slightly more grace.

Maria's voice swallowed her up. If she had been talentless, she would have been plump. She would have had children. She would have found peace between her ears.

She had that fat proud nose, and she liked to stare down it. Her hair was thick, and it required long bouts with the brush.

One night she swallowed too many pills, and I called the doctor, the discreet one, and he pumped the rancid stew from her belly. When she woke, she was quite angry with me.

She had not performed in many months.

"Is this the way you treat me?" she asked. "Is this how you repay me?"

She asked these things repeatedly, for several minutes. Eventually, I grew tired of these words. They meant nothing. I cooed at her, shushed her. Her words continued. They were slowed and partially drugged.

Eventually, I played one of her recordings, a performance of *Norma*, on the phonograph. That stopped her complaints. She listened to herself.

She began to sing. It sounded like two women in the midst of a furious quarrel. They fought over the song.

Maria could be funny. Would you have guessed that?

I once asked her, "Why can't you be in a funny opera?"

She said, "They're all funny. I consider every one a comedy in which only I know the joke."

Even *Norma.* This may be the truest thing she ever spoke. She peered down her long fat nose at me. I was kneeling to hem a dress. I had three mending pins pressed between my lips, and they tasted like spite. We both nodded. Her eyes folded away under her skin. This was an unusual truth for her. Most of her truths came only under duress or the influence of song.

The joke of *Norma* is its urgency. Night haunts the sacred forest. That's how *Norma* begins. It's about druids and vows and secrets and children and sacrifices of blood. The plot spins. It tangles you up. In the beginning—or is it the end?—Norma plans to slaughter her own children. Sometimes as Maria sang, she seemed quite unhappy about this.

There's much more, too. Betrayals. Foolish love. Foolish hate. Death hangs on every word, and then perhaps Norma sacrifices herself. The ladies and the gentlemen clap and clap and clap until their deaf hands grow bruised with commotion. They stand, they clap some more, they put on their velvet wraps, they straighten their brows, and they go home and drink a glass of wine and think noble thoughts about the purity of motherhood. They never consider the fact that Norma was joking, that she went home, too, and had several glasses of wine and didn't think about much of anything except the itch of her own desires.

Of course, Maria had to please thousands of people, and I only had to please her.

There are those who like to swirl their ideas around the glass. Gossip dyes their teeth purple. They drink deeply and say she had Onassis's baby.

I listened through the walls. This wasn't eavesdropping. It wasn't by choice. Onassis was the kind of man who liked to take up space in your head. He yelled out for what he wanted, and he seldom yelled twice. I heard a great deal of yelling from him and from her, and I heard the noise of pleasure and the squeal of pain.

There is solstice in another's body, but it comes with the price of another's armpits and another's tobacco lips and another's toes fermenting in socks.

Perhaps she listened on the other side of the wall, too.

Night haunts the sacred forest, and the tiny bones thrum in our ears, and it's a small miracle of anatomy.

Once, in Paris, in the third act of *Norma*, Maria tried to hit a high note, and it cracked like a frozen stick snapping in two. Half the audience clapped, cheered with a generous pity, and half screeched at her. Maria gazed at all of us. She made a stabbing motion at the conductor. The orchestra began the part again. Maria sang anew. She hit the high note, and she held it for each of us to admire. It did not crack.

The entire house screamed for her. The clapping echoed like a lover breaking down a bedroom door. She needed those noises of love. But she died almost alone, without Onassis, without a crowd.

Without an audience, she felt quite ill with the world.

Maria had appetites. I had serving utensils, sharpened knives. I trimmed the beef into crimson ribbons.

And after she died, I jabbed the knife into the marble countertop. Over and over. The metal clashed with rock, chipped away. I believe I was etching a monument, though I am not sure if it marked her death or her life. I couldn't help. As The Great Thinker tells us, We die swaddled in our lonely souls.

The journalist smelled like a lilac stubbed out in an ashtray. He sat close enough so that I could see inside his mind. It was a careless mind, cluttered.

"Could you tell me more?" he asked.

"There's no more."

He said, "I think there is."

I said, "Cluttered mind."

He said, "Tell me about Onassis's baby."

His voice was the husk of a husk.

"There was no baby."

"Not true," he said.

He reached over and pinched the fat loose flesh of my inner thigh, centimeters from my womanhood. I felt a wicked rush of pink heat, fear, near-joy, thirst.

"You are not a gentleman," I said.

He pinched me again. Harder. Later, I discovered that he left two purpled welts. We waited. I took the scent of him in, and it settled on my tongue. His breath was deep and syrupy, and I could feel him leaning in, leaning in, leaning in. His fingers were ready.

He said, "Tell me, old woman."

The father of this boy wasn't a butcher. He was a tenor. That's all I'll say. He slipped into my bed in the dark of night, and I made him leave before the dawn opened her mouth to sneer at us. I was perhaps rougher with him than he expected. He yelped as if our act were painful, and he said stop, stop, don't stop, stop. It grew tiresome. I never summoned him back to the pleasures of my bed.

All in all, we are simply raw meat served up for the world's teeth. I've felt those bites, seen their progress on my body. My knees don't bend the way they should, and my fingers play clumsy tricks on me. Here is my cup of tea decorating the floor. Here is my sewing needle lost to my eyes. Here is the lock on the door that takes me eight tries to open. These are all the jokes told by my nibbled fingers. The world chews us up.

Maria knew this. She chewed back. She had an appetite. This was her natural way. She has been dead now for twenty-eight years. My hairs grow thick with gray and white, and they sprout out of the oddest places. A few ring my ears, and I enlist the patient minutes to pluck them out. But Maria hasn't aged in all this time. Now, the relationship works.

We could have been sisters. She was only two years younger than I was, but I chose to make her my daughter. She made me comfortable but not rich, but that is not why I adopted her. One does not adopt to acquire riches. One adopts to acquire blood.

My daughter is moldy bones and dirt and many, many records, all that recorded sound. If you listen to the phonograph, you know it's not real. She's not in the next room. But we all have ways of fooling ourselves. I only had to fool her (and myself), but she had to fool everyone.

I fashioned her into a daughter, and the baby, dead on arrival so many years ago, is too young to be my son. It is the gift I give to her.

When I had the baby, I was lost to needles and adrift between sleep and this world. I asked her, "Did you see it?"

She said, "He had fine black hair like the feathers of a crow, and if you tried, you could imagine that he slept."

Night haunts the sacred forest, and sometimes my eyes want to play tricks. It's the cataracts. They reverse the sky like a photographic negative. In that sheet of night whiteness, each of those black stars could be a period, the death of my words.

All those periods require words. But they hate words, too.

She was my daughter, and when she was hungry, I fed her. I consoled her, and I fed her, and I tucked her in, and I fed her, and I trimmed her hairs, and I fed her, and I rubbed her fat back, and I made her honeyed black tea, and I fed her, filling her stomach, saving her from emptiness, even on days when the meat was gray and dour, even when it required a fragrant sauce to fool the tongue.

In heaven/hell/the dirt, I will wait on her again. I will wait on her, on the spoiled-pumpkin soldier, on the baby, on the butchers, on the tenor, on the journalist.

I told him that Maria had this baby, a secret, a stillborn.

"Did you see the baby?" the journalist asked.

"He had fine black hair like the feathers of a crow," I said, "and if you tried, you could imagine that he slept."

When I think about this boy, I see a squiggle of flesh, pink and raw. He is not a human thing. He swirls, and he snarls, and he feasts upon my liver, the tender parts of my brain. He's free to swim up through my chest. I created him. He slithers and demands his rewards, his fresh meat. Even now, I feel the throb of him in my guts.

This worm beckons, but I can keep him at bay.

She would forgive me. She would say, Forget all this. She would say, Scratch your desires.

When my stuttering butcher appears tomorrow, I will lure him into bed. I am wizened but not brittle, and parts of myself still have ways of speaking lewdly. If my ears can forgive him, his eyes can forgive me, and he, too, is old, although not as old as I, and he, too, doesn't always fit into the contours of this world. I will tweak his mustache, and I will sing for him, and I will rub the gristled parts of him that can come alive with blood. I will show him my bruises. We will share the joke of urgency. But I must hurry. And he must hurry. And the night must hurry. And the world, too.

THE CHEZ DU PANCAKES

TIANANMEN BENT DOWN before the The Chez du Pancakes as if he were praying.

Then we saw the flames.

When he ran down the street, churning away from the juts of smoke, we ran as well. We were a great mob designed to bring him comfort.

Except maybe this is the end of the story.

We tend to get ahead of ourselves sometimes. Then we smash and bump into one another. We elbow and push. Beer gets spilled. We suffer bruised feelings and body parts. Swearing spreads like the heebakibees. All in all it's bad for the esprit de corps.

So we'll take it slow, single file, and if that's the case, Tiananmen must come first.

Tiananmen is the one who moved across the seas and opened a bar and hoisted a beacon: a sign that said The Chez du Pancakes. We just went in and ordered waffles.

Tiananmen said, "We have no waffles," and poured us a pitcher of beer.

The dream began; it startled us out of our stupor. Our desire for waffles had been flawed, even silly. We talked about dreams, strong strapping dreams that were also delicious; they had spines and whipped toppings.

Tiananmen said, "My dream is to become an American of sorts."

We told him America was just the place to do it.

We had advice for him: We told him how India Indians own hotels and Pakistanis own convenience stores. We suggested he say, "Give me some skin," when he wished to slap our various hands. We urged him to sponsor a Little League team, and the wee nippers went 12-0. Tiananmen had touched them, too. He had lovingly clothed them in uncomfortable polyester.

We offered him grammar tips: We said the passive voice should never be used by him.

We displayed empathy: We assured him that it was OK to be vertically challenged. It was OK to be a foreigner. It was OK to be just about anything. We explained that we would only mention these things—dissect them and mock them—behind his tiny little back.

In all honesty, we asked things of Tiananmen that we would never ask of ourselves. Mainly we begged for free drinks.

We were all tattooed, hungry, waffleless, riddled with sin, diseased and generous with it. Sixty percent of us were overweight. Tiananmen pointed this out to us in a newspaper article; we paged ahead to the TV listings.

When we ran out on our tabs, he chased us into the parking lot, menaced us with politeness, and we paid him with the dollars that had been mashed deep into our pockets, with the change we hid in our car ashtrays.

Sometimes he said, "I'm not deaf, you know."

Sometimes he said something under his breath, which we figured was chanting.

Sometimes he got all Zen-like on us.

Mistakes were made: It came to our attention that, apparently, Tiananmen was not from *China* China. How were we supposed to know, particularly after we started calling him Tiananmen? He was from Taiwan. Was there really a difference? There was some sort of difference, which he explained several times.

We were interested in his culture and customs. We watched him drive and asked where he had been practicing. We begged him to burp in the Asian way. We tried to figure out Taiwanese swear words. Sadly, he had not eaten dog.

Could he do math? We called him The Abacus. And then we started calling him Tiananmen, and we noticed he used a calculator, which made us think the whole math question was superfluous and beneath us.

He spread out our cultural horizon as if it were peanut butter. We considered bringing foreign exchange students into our homes, where they could bask in Americanness, share their rich cultural weirdnesses, and do household chores, yard work, baby-sitting.

Despite all this, all those nights at the bar, all the bodily fluids we had spilled and he had seen, we didn't think we knew him. We didn't think he knew the real us, the softer side, the furry underbelly, the underpants.

When the bar closed that night, we took him to a party.

He said, "I need to go home."

We said he needed to come try our American customs: the beer bong, the body shot, the hash pipe, frozen burritos sizzling in the microwave. We pulled him into the backseat with us. We would not take "fuck no" for an answer.

We threw gang signs and made Irish toasts about the road popping you in the face and sunshine and freckles and SPF 45. We chased Tiananmen around the room and gave him various wrestling-mat-related hugs. We administered wedgies. How much did we love him? Enough to make him physically uncomfortable.

Then Tiananmen made a speech.

He said, "I hate your nipping sausage fingers."

He said, "I hate how you drink too much beer and wear ball caps. You yell like fat braying hyenas, except with flossed teeth."

Some of us sucked our minty bicuspids. Some of us stopped yelling. Some of us adjusted our ball caps. With the bills turned 180 degrees, we were more cosmopolitan, citizens of the world. Or, at the very least, catchers.

But Tiananmen wouldn't stop.

He said, "You all sail yachts and eat pork rinds."

We burped in unison.

He said, "You are insider traders and zit poppers and alley pissers and tax cheaters: I believe these truths to be self-evident."

At that point, we had no idea of anything except how his voice sputtered and strained and crashed into random words.

We patiently explained that some of us were not wearing ball caps. Some of us were allergic to pork rinds. Some of us did not piss in the alley. Yachts were for rich jerks.

"Yes, yes, yes," he said.

He said, "My good god, in my own way I have become one of you."

We weren't sure who his good god was. Allah? Buddha? But we cheered anyway. He was part of us now. We told him this.

He said, "That's horrible."

We laughed at his malapropism.

He said, "We must go to The Chez du Pancakes."

We followed him back to the bar, to the dream. We were single file, caring, respectful, united by shared beliefs and the possibility of free after-hours beer.

Tiananmen bent down before The Chez du Pancakes as if he were praying.

Then we saw the flames.

When he ran down the street, churning away from the juts of smoke, we ran as well. We were a great mob designed to bring him comfort.

BOY, SEA, BOY

THE SEA OFFERED BITS of spite, parts of the ship. All splinters. First Mate waited for something of substance, a dead body, his chess set, buildable wood. The sea offered none of these things.

First Mate neither cried nor mourned. He had hated them all—Captain with his lispy orders, Sebastian with his receding hairline, a head like a cobwebbed egg; he could supply more too, more people, more reasons to hate—and had the ship not sunk he himself would have offered his own flesh to the sea. He would have said, "Here is a body and here are bones and here is a spleen and here is a headache and here is a swan dive." Instead he found himself on an island, and here is a body, living, First Mate's body, and here are seagulls and here are trees and here are memory's noises and here are the splinters slurped up on the beach.

The morning when the boy walked out of the water, First Mate questioned himself, these splinters, his state. It was a dream except for the salt smell of the sea, except for the loud conflict of wave meeting beach, except for the boy standing before him crying, blowing snot, taking large dangerous swallows of air.

He did not act but gave thought to embracing the boy, who was clothed in canvas pants, who was coated with salt and seawater. The boy had thick black curly hair, a face with the shape and tone of a Bosc pear, eyes black and lost.

The boy drank from the air, spat a small brackish puddle onto the beach. The boy looked at him, spat again, began to run toward the forest. First Mate followed him with his eyes. The boy ran so fast his legs flared in harsh and awkward angles.

First Mate yelled, "Stop!"

The boy did not pause, did not look back. He disappeared into the trees.

First Mate found a comfortable spot where the forest met the beach. He let his fingers pick through his own thick black curly hair. He scratched his face that was the shape and tone of a Bosc pear. He closed his eyes, hid the evidence that they were black and lost. He sat under a tree and began to wait.

He wondered, puzzled the puzzle in his mind.

The sky pulled its shades over the day, and still the boy would not come out.

"Stubborn, stubborn beast," First Mate said.

First Mate fashioned himself a bed of dirt, collapsed by the edge of the forest, let sleep poke a hole in his thoughts where the dreams dripped in, then out.

He woke up empty.

In the morning, First Mate thrashed through the trees, the brush, the stingers that nestled under his skin. The boy had disappeared, most likely up a tree. First Mate yelled for him, "Boy, boy, boy. Come out."

First Mate offered mangos and his last prized speck of salted beef. He hollered. He thrashed bushes with a heavy stick. Finally, he spotted a pant leg hanging out of a lush leafy branch.

As First Mate tugged on the leg, the boy wiggled, fought, yelped. But First Mate had the advantages of firm footing and bulk. Soon, the resistance melted, and the boy crashed to the earth.

On his left forearm, the boy had the familiar coffee-brown stain; from certain angles it looked like a spider. First Mate had covered up his spider mark years ago. It was obliterated by a tattoo of a sailing ship that rocked on the inky waves of First Mate's arm hair. The boy, of course, could not read the skin below this ship, the boy did not know the flesh they shared, and First Mate smiled at this advantage.

"How old are you now?" First Mate asked.

The boy held up nine fingers.

First Mate had to tramp through the uneven ground of memory.

First Mate said, "Do you remember last year, when Madame Ostella caught you stealing those cakes? She sliced you open with a hemlock switch. It hurt for several days, and you only ate one of the cakes, and it tasted like soap."

The boy offered his wide black eyes, two spots of tar adrift in a face.

First Mate said, "One should never eat stolen cakes. You're a bad little silent boy. I don't like looking into your soul like this, but I will if I have to. I have an island, its purity to protect."

The boy squished up his right eye and looked at First Mate with his left. Cheekiness. As if he were measuring First Mate for a carpentry project.

First Mate would do the building here. He would build respect and fear and answers.

"How long were you in the sea?" First Mate asked.

The boy squawked out the words. First Mate knew what this tone meant, the desperation of unpracticed lies, the way they constricted young vocal cords.

"I was there for three days," the boy said. "I caught fish with my hands, and collected rocks, and collected pebbles, and I ate raw things out of their shells."

"Mollusks."

"Raw things. I couldn't hear anything, and I got sick of the salt, and I got bored."

"You didn't like it?"

"I liked it, just not enough. I lived with a woman with a fish's tail."

"I know all your stories. Don't you lie to me."

"She had golden hair, and she sang, but I couldn't hear it. She wanted me to follow her, to live in the sea."

"Lies and more lies."

First Mate knew he had told fibs like these. How he had been kidnapped by gypsies, how a beautiful woman with wings stole his boots, how the coins he had been given to buy milk dissolved in his fingers.

He said, "Boy, have you ever seen coins dissolve in your hands?"

"Just once. The milk money."

First Mate savored this. He closed his eyes, marched back through time again, remembered Madame Ostella's face perverted with unbelieving fury.

He said, "Boy, do you remember the green vein dancing in her head?"

He expected them to share the triumph of the popping vein. He himself could see Madame Ostella, so angry but so unable to stop him.

When he opened his eyes, the boy bolted, scampered through a prickly bush.

First Mate had forgotten what an insolent little prig he had been. Elusive too. The boy would find a better hiding place this time. The boy would adapt to the environment, sink into it, and that made First Mate's task, his entire day, harder, pricklier, sweatier.

First Mate found a large hard cudgel of wood, and as the day fried his skin, as the hiding boy fried his patience, he smashed through the bushes, rapped on tree branches, poked his weapon into caves and gullies. As First Mate thrashed through the forest, the dirt clung to him, and his hair was alive with grease and sweat and flies. First Mate had so much to teach the boy. He would have to shake the boy until his bones understood. He would have to be harsh because the world demanded this quality.

Exhausted and empty, First Mate had demands, too. He needed the ocean's cool mercy—it would chill his thoughts—and there the boy stood, near the water's edge.

The boy held a fragment of coconut and scratched at it, stabbed it with a stick. The boy was killing the coconut shell, torturing the thing. Then the boy stopped. The stick was jammed into the center of the coconut shard, and the boy calmly walked into the water. As the boy waded out into the surf, let go of the coconut, First Mate saw it from a different perspective: It floated. A boat.

First Mate had made his own boats out of folded newspaper and sent them coursing down the flooded street gutters. Those paper boats soaked it all in, acquired coats of mud, were ripped up by older boys, and even when they sailed, they inevitably sogged or crumpled.

First Mate turned his mind to the craft of stealth. He was down near the water's edge before the boy spotted him.

First Mate said, "I know what you're thinking. You would like to see a naked woman walk out of the water, see her shake the wetness from her body."

The boy held his dripping boat in his hands now and sneered up at First Mate.

One after the other, the boy spit out his words, *ptew, ptew, ptew,* like so many black watermelon seeds of hate: "I know about you, too. You beat up that woman, the one in the green dress, after you took off your clothes, after you slumped on top of her, after you gave her money. You beat her up, and you took your money back.

"You pushed that sailor overboard, and you didn't tell anyone.

"You steered the ship into that rock."

First Mate chased the boy deeper into the water. He hollered at him. He said, "Come back and eat your fists and eat your words and eat your sins."

The boy plunged headfirst into the surf. He pumped his arms like a windup swimmer, a tin automaton. He would rust and corrode, and his parts would seize up.

The water burned into First Mate's skin with its icicle flame.

He wasn't a strong swimmer. This he knew. Everybody knew. The other orphans would pantomime throwing him into the river and laugh great hearty hollers. It wasn't funny. He would overcome this. He would swim out and grab the boy and pull him back to the island and throttle him.

He would scar the boy's hide with thorn branches. He would make the boy's ears sing with bitter songs. He would tame his own flesh.

He forced himself farther and farther from the shore, into a great wavy depth. He could see the wet fur of the boy's head bobbing off in the distance.

First Mate cursed the boy, cursed the sea, spit in it, flailed his arms in it, kicked it, again and again and again. Swallowed a large choking mouthful of it.

His fists spoke to him, and the sea spoke its great crashing talk, too.

First Mate saw a succession of fists at the orphanage. He saw a schoolmarm's hand clapping harshly over his ear. On certain cloudy days, that ear rang, a shrill spinster whistle that only he could hear. He saw Madame Ostella pressing his hand into a scalding teakettle. He remembered a fat old man who smelled like burnt matches stuffing a hand into First Mate's trousers. The old man's touch felt like some new cruel handshake. He remembered being stabbed in the thigh by a shopkeeper. It didn't bleed much, seeped a little. The scar was a disappointment, not really the kind of thing to show off.

The waves shook him up and down. He saw boy, sea, boy. Then all he saw was open sea.

He said a little prayer to himself, some other form of himself, his best self, and then he was thrashing against the undertow.

For a second, a wave flipped him onto his back, and in the sky, he saw a demented egg, round and angry with light. What a thing it would be to step on it, crush the glowing shell, make it bleed its runny yolk.

First Mate thrashed with more specific effort. He couldn't see the boy anymore. The surf had swallowed the child. The boy was with his fish-tailed woman. She had golden hair, and she sang in a silent language from the depths.

THE KIDS

PAUL CHASED them away.

"Get out of here," he yelled.

They scattered. Four of them running off, howling in the dark. The green plastic can was tipped onto its side, its innards spilled out and all over the patio behind the garage.

Paul looked at scraps of used napkins, a pile of something vaguely larval, traces of white paste (mayonnaise? chunkified sour milk?). In theory, it was abstract expressionism, but it possessed a message of pure lucidity: "You are now required to re-gather your own waste products, punkass fool!"

He swept up, and the trash stenched through his nostrils, came to rest as a skunked-beer tang on his tongue.

The cartilage snapped in his knees, and he trudged into the house, down the hall, into the den.

"The kids again," he said.

Crystal did not look up. The television shuddered and enticed. Her finger pecked at the remote, and he sucked on the inside of his mouth until the hoppy dirt taste slipped away. She clicked into the inevitable future: the next highest channel, then into darkness, a static peace.

"Tomorrow night," she said, "we get those punkingtons."

He went out to the garage to hammer the night away, let Crystal work on her online classes (Communications Law and Ethics). Out in the garage, he had tools and a stash of white bread. Tasteless really. Just mash it around with a minimum of teeth. The slices contained nothing, empty calories, the band of fat around Paul's middle. He kept a loaf or two in an empty paint can, a dried puddle of green on the bottom, contraband above. He pounded away at random nails, glowered over dowels, banished the carbohydrate cravings.

They liked to imagine them as devils, beasts, roaring little gnomes.

Crystal said, "They're half teenager, half raccoon."

He said, "Half goat, half pain in the ass."

She said, "They do it to the Smythes, too."

He said, "Take off your nightgown."

She pulled it up, revealing her legs, vaguely unshaven, then her pale belly, flat hard breasts. The material snagged around her head and chin, and then she wrestled the gown over and off her head. A puckered smile sprang out at him.

He said, "Come to bed."

She said, "Pants off, too."

Crystal shook the hamburger until the patty slithered out of its bun.

Paul said, "I hate this part. What's a little bun done to you?"

She de-bunned several more burgers, said, "Eat, Dr. Atkins." She patted the rubbery mound of flesh under his T-shirt.

Paul said, "Don't call me Dr. Fatkins."

They filled themselves with protein and cheesy fat.

He watched her jaw open, rapidly piston, open again to take in another bite, and then more furious pistoning, as if the burger were a problem best dealt with quickly. He poked at charred meat with the tine of his fork.

He peered at her black eyes and her spiked hair; she looked like a little punky elf. He knew she liked to fool people, let them think she was small and bitter. Then she was bright, shiny almost, and enthusiastic and talking out of a mouthful of gristle.

"Tonight, we hide out. We hide in the garage, and when the kids come to knock over the trash, we pop out and scare the shit out of them. Call some parents, squeeze some tears out of stoned heads."

He nodded down his burger.

She said, "There's boiled eggs all ready for breakfast."

The smallest one ran the second-fastest, and they realized later that this had been an error in judgment, a silly assumption that he would be the slowest. First, Paul had stumbled out of the door, caught his foot on something, then they had chased the wrong one. But Crystal had watched carefully, rewound the blunders in her memory, picked at them until they offered improvements, new tactics.

"The middle one, he's the fastest, so he's out. Small one's quick, too. The two big ones, we get the one that runs sort-of-sideways. You saw him. He had on the lime-green jacket and jeans. Ran funny. Slow. He's the one. They're all skinny twerps. We get Limey next time. Grab him. You need to wear better shoes, sneakers maybe."

Paul remembered an explosion of shrieking children, as if four of them had become eight. Legs thrashing, garish jackets. Skinny arms a-pumping. What kind of boy wore cotton-candy pink? Lime Green was the best bet. Nice and slow. Catchable.

In the break room, Paul dropped his quarters into the machine.

"Look," he said, "I know I'm not supposed to, but I'm just going to have this Hostess. A little chocolate, a little puff of cream, that's it."

Veronica said, "It's like four and a half pounds. I'm serious. It's a sin almost."

Veronica, of course, was on the Atkins, too. She had lost thirteen pounds, traded meatloaf recipes with Crystal.

Paul looked at Veronica's thinned-out seriousness, her baggy herringbone pants cinched with a belt. She was practically lithe, green-eyed, joyless. He was at least two of her, two and a half of Crystal.

"You can hate the sin," he said, "but love the sinner, baby. Just don't tell my wife."

Veronica said, "Why don't you go eat that in your cubicle?"

Paul ran his fingers through his long blond-gray hair, said, "I'm getting to be an old hippie." Slapped his belly for emphasis.

She said, "Just leave that thing alone."

Crystal pulled his hair back into a ponytail, yanked it firmly, not cruelly, and then ran the elastic ring up the bundle of hair.

He said, "Will you do that temple thing?"

She rubbed small intense circles into his fleshy head.

He said, "What are those things called? Snickeroodles?"

She said, "Doodles."

He said, "Man, snickerdoodles and bagels and those big pouffy muffins with the chocolate chips."

"Enough. Even I'm about drooling."

"Big pieces of blueberry pie. You zap it for like thirty seconds, and then the ice cream melts over everything."

She said, "Stop it already."

They heard the sound of kids violating their trash, and this time Paul was Niked and swift. He felt a roaring brain confluence of adrenaline and oxygen.

He didn't have to go more than six big strides and he was next to the fallen target, a pile of lime-green polyester, skinniness, crazy hair. The boy was holding his leg with one hand, half of a hamburger bun with the other.

Crystal said, "What the fuck do you think you're doing?"

The boy looked at the hamburger bun as if it would supply the answer. A portion of bun was missing. A mouthful. A half-dollar-sized taste.

Crystal said, "Where did you get that?"

The leg hand abandoned its post, pointed at the tipped can, the ripped garbage bag. Paul peered at his trash, sniffed at it, the spoiled ketchupy rot.

The boy's flesh stuck close to his bones. His eyes hid deep in his skull. He made a wispy sound through his nose, went back to holding his leg. I'm as big as five of these kids, Paul thought, five and a half. Six was pushing it.

Paul said, "Maybe you ought to go home now."

Crystal pulled the boy to his feet. She said, "What's your name? Where do you live?"

He mumbled some syllables toward them.

They watched the boy limp into the night.

Paul said, "This isn't something I'm really proud of."

She said, "In the morning, I'm calling everybody and their fucking lawyers."

The state had all these agencies, and Paul read their names to her from the Yellow Pages, then a trail of numbers. She argued with computerized menus, pressed buttons, harassed voicemail boxes, finally got through to someone at the Division of Youth and Family Services, yelled at him, bullied him.

She said, "I'm going over there, and you're coming with me."

Paul said, "I'm going under duress."

"I'm just doing things mechanically," she said, and she inserted her tab-A arm into the slot-B crook of his.

The morning dredged them with mist, and they took a short damp walk to the address, waited out in the street for the Family Services people. Two cruisers and a Nissan arrived, and Paul and Crystal watched a tribe of crew cuts, an officious balding man, and a short golden-haired woman march into the house.

They plucked the kids out two at a time. The children waved to Paul and Crystal. Paul started to wave, stopped, began again. The crew cuts returned to the house. The kids were stuffed into the Nissan. Circus clowns, Paul thought. Paul lurked on the sidewalk. Crystal went over, talked to the Family Services guy, who had a clipboard and a glinting moist bald spot. Paul saw Crystal's head bob up and down, uh-huh, uh-huh, and then the guy's shook back and forth. They challenged each other with their incompatible head wobbles. Then Crystal reached out, grabbed the guy, hugged him roughly. He tried to step back from her, stunned a bit maybe, not quite intoxicated but fucked up on this, her arms around him like a corset of flesh.

He said, "All right, all right already."

This Paul heard from way out in the street. The Family Services guy got the four kids out of the car. They were all kindling-limbed, sunken-faced, painfully small. Lime Green now wore a blue hoodie that swallowed up his hands. She hugged them one at a time. She enveloped them in her arms, lifted them for a second off the earth, let them hover and kick. She squished their torsos and patted backs. They seemed to want the ground back. The short blond Family Services woman dug her sensible feet into the lawn; she wore a look of violent impatience. Paul could hear her, too.

"This will never do," she said. "Never do."

Their feet worked, brought Paul and Crystal home. Their tongues simply quit.

Finally Crystal said, "I'm calling in sick."

They bought all the papers, even the tabloids, read all the horrible little words.

How old the boys were, nineteen looking like ten, ten looking like six. How they were all foster children. How the boys had scarfed wallboard and insulation, anything to fill their stomachs.

Paul said, "They had to eat fucking houses."

The boys had starved out in the open, in church, on the street, on Paul and Crystal's street, and reporters had variously described Paul and Crystal as "shocked," "amazed," "wounded," "befuddled."

Crystal said, "I don't like knowing how the reporters think I feel. I don't like reading about it."

The phone rang and rang and bleated until Paul unhooked the receiver and muffled it, shut it away forever in the silverware drawer.

On the TV, a haggard Family Services spokesman said, "The system is designed to protect children, but even the best systems possess a degree of failure."

In a few months, the spokesman said, the children would be placed in new and loving foster homes; the system would prevail.

Crystal clicked the remote to off.

Paul said, "Months from now, no one's going to remember those kids."

"Except for us," she said.

At work, Veronica pressed him, tried to get him to spit out the details.

She said, "Did their stomachs stick out? Distended maybe? That's what the *Post* said."

He spooned chocolate pudding out of a little plastic cup, scraped all the goop out of it.

He said, "I'm not talking about it. It's over."

Paul looked at her hard-boned arms, her collapsing waist. She's belted like a radial, he thought.

She said, "Those Family Services people are going to roast on spits."

When he came home from work early, just 3:15, Crystal's body was plopped randomly on the couch. Head in the middle, feet hanging over the armrest.

She said, "Big lovely man."

He said, "You drunk?"

Crystal said, "It's gin. It's kosher. Atkinsosher."

He said, "Hand that bottle over here. I need a coupla-three drinks myself."

She said, "No lime, no tonic."

At twilight, she followed him down the driveway. He punched the code, and the big garage door of his workshop skittered up and open: a giant mouth that sucked them in. Then he pushed the code again, and the mouth closed, trapping them for a second in half-dark. His dull-eyed hands found the light switch, turned it on.

"Maybe off," she said.

He called back the gray, and they stood in it as their eyes mellowed and then sharpened.

They had decided to keep the cans there.

She said, "Let's do it."

Earlier, he had grappled the heavier one into the center of the garage. She ran at it, pushed, smashed it over, puffed and yelled, "Damn you."

The can belched out its trash-bag guts.

He kicked at the bag, over and over, until it broke open, surrendered its filth and a burping sound, a tang of vinegar cut with bacon grease. She kicked at the pile, thrashed, brought up last week's newspapers, coffee grounds, eggshells, Kleenexes, paper towels, aluminum cans.

She kicked, kicked, kicked, unearthed a dirt-stained greeting card from under a pile of pencil shavings and snarls of hair. The card said, "Hope you're feeling Beeyootiful!" She said, "Christ, Christ, Christ."

He said, "Crap."

She said, "Feel this. Feel it."

They stomped, pulverized. She climbed on the knocked-over can, squatted on top until the open end of the green plastic bowed into a leer.

He felt a film of wet heat between his shirt and his skin. His heart buckled and then pumped even quick spurts. He pounded a stray hamburger bun under his foot until it became a soupy pulp.

She said, "They liked our trash the best. They told me."

He straightened his body, asked, "Why the goddamn hell?" He stretched his arms up and out until his back answered with a sharp pop.

He winced himself into a slouch.

From the workbench, he took the old paint can where he hid the Wonder Bread, pushed a screwdriver down into the gap, pried off the metal lid, showed her his carbohydrate stash.

She said, "You're a big fat sneak."

He said, "You don't mean that."

"Probably I don't." She didn't apologize.

He untwisted the bag, pulled out perfect twin squares, canvases of pure processed wheat with golden brown frames.

He said, "We're in this fucking world together, all of it."

They stuffed the pieces into their mouths. They ripped it with their teeth, tore at it. It was all tender bruisable flesh.

They became devils, beasts, roaring little gnomes.

When the bread was gone, mashed by teeth, festering in the body's internal logic of acid and renewal, she chipped inside the can with the screwdriver, dug away at the residue lurking at the bottom of the can. She loosed two dime-sized slivers of dried-up sea green, the color of their front door, the shutters.

They took these little pills together. He pressed his paint chip under his tongue, tasted a sweetness burning in his saliva. She sat on the bowed can. Her eyes challenged and forgave him. She had swallowed hers, opened her mouth to prove it.

BLACK BOX

THE MISSION OVERFLOWS with false angels and the sting of broken teeth. Our missing parts yell at us. My molar aches from a distant landfill, and the ghosts we never believed in tug at our sleeves, stare us down, keep us on a trajectory we did not choose. I imagine voices from the clouds. They sing and beg me to join in on the chorus.

"Bumps, hitches, errors, evil spirits, and pants filled with shit," I say.

M. says, "A., shut your thesaurus mouth."

Far below, the Sears Tower mocks us. It's a giant middle finger stuck up in the fist of Chicago. As we float beyond it, M. cranes his neck to look. I curse both Sears and Roebuck.

"There goes the thing we were supposed to destroy," M. says.

M.'s face is swollen with peanuts, busted pride, and the urge to do more violence: It fills his eyes with tributaries of blood. We are in the cockpit, the pilots and copilots are dead, the flight attendants are cowed, the passengers are filled with awe and vomit, the air marshal is dead, S. is dead, W. is dead, T. is dead, I am at the controls, and M. chews, alternately, on honey-roasted snacks and the tips of his fingers.

"Fly this fucker, motherfucker," M. says.

S. was a sweaty motherfucker, and W. was a pissy motherfucker, and I am a stupid motherfucker. With M. the adjectives change, but the motherfucker always remains.

He says, "We will continue the mission."

M. summons a flight attendant, the plump brownish one with the tits. She brings him another beer. As he drinks, the can loses strength; the aluminum surrenders its shape to his fingers.

"Such a leader."

M. says, "Shhh. The black box hears everything."

It is his fourteenth beer. The world requires coping mechanisms. Our comrades are dead, and the world is stuck on pause. The airliner will neither dive nor ascend. Its course appears locked, predetermined, timeless. The instruments don't waver, not even the fuel gauges. This is the fourteenth hour of this no-time, no-choice, no-change. At least we think so. Our watches are frozen, too. A perpetual 9:37 of the soul.

"I'm going to drop a fatwa on your ass," M. says.

He doesn't believe in this overwhelming stasis. I believe. The plane is destined for something; it is beyond our control.

We are somewhere high above Illinois.

M. shuffles through his beloved almanac.

He says, "Instead, we will destroy the home of the Green Bay Packers."

M. is an upset stomach multiplied by itself deposited in your head and yelling. This, of course, is only when he is on his best behavior.

He punched me in the mouth once, two years ago, and I spit up a nugget of molar. He drove me to the dentist, waited in the little room, leered at the receptionist as I was drilled and patched. Out in the parking lot, he punched me again.

"It is stronger now, you see."

He was proud of how he had reinforced my teeth.

For nine years and two months, M. never slept. He stayed up nights squinting at the shopping channels and planning our glorious attack.

We should have had families and children and lice scares and mortgages and microwave popcorn and pet rodents. We are the angels of death. The angels of death take no spouses. They acquire no hamsters.

M. is the deadliest angel. He sits next to me, and he's as drunk as a cannibal.

As an experiment, I tug with all my arm-muscle energy on the throttle. The part moves violently. The aircraft offers no response.

We can't dive, and the altitude never changes, and everything stays so far away. Our goals are distant and prickly.

M. leafs through his almanac.

He says, "New target: Mount Rushmore."

I say, "There's a movie, 'Rushmore.'"

M. says, "Bill Murray."

He drinks another beer. His anger turns heavy-lidded. He has a tanned face shaped like a mango. His eyes do a googly dance, and his tongue searches for his lips. His mustache looks almost dainty.

From the back of the plane, I hear the bloody-voiced man scream, "We will be saved. All of us."

M. says, "Bill Murray."

Although M. starts to spit up little streams of lemony vomit, he does not seem terribly concerned.

He says, "Malmush."

And he closes his fat-veiled eyes.

I summon the stewardess, and I order another beverage service for the passengers.

It is the plump one again. Her face has a dampish sheen, which glows and drips. Sweat and fear, we all wear these things.

She asks, "Is he passed out?"

I say, "He is napping."

When she leaves the cockpit, I experiment with the controls.

The turn coordinator won't budge. I check every needle. The altimeter doesn't waver. The vertical speed indicator supplies an eerie flatness. The compass aligns the same old earth. All these lights, all these needles, all these dials, all these switches, all these swears in my head.

Nothing. No motion. I have no control. I check again, for the 357th time; the autopilot functions are disengaged.

I say, "M., I heard you listening to that Tupac Shakur album. I saw you embracing that hoochie mama. I know you ate W.'s frozen veggie burgers."

He snorts like a Chia Pet.

M. doesn't listen, and the stewardesses don't listen, and Reginald Harshbeck didn't listen, and the air marshal didn't listen.

Only the black box listens.

Black Box, we were the slackers and outcasts.

We weren't good enough for the first mission. We lacked fanaticism, order, strength of will, control of our own bladders. How many days clicked past, how many times did we think of our own glorious exploding plane? Nine years and two months worth of days. We trained with laptop flight simulators. We asked where our glory was. We waited. We grew older. We acquired video games and pension plans.

I worked for the last five years at Microsoft. To Reginald Harshbeck, he of the next cubicle and the hairy knuckles, I say fuck yourself and also your wastebasket.

For nine years and two months, we assimilated and Americanized and worried and hid in plain sight and waited. Worried, worried, worried. Worried about capture. Worried about failure. Worried about revenge. Waited, waited, waited. All that brain-cracking waiting.

Nine years, two months, after the first go-round, and here I am, and here is M. half drunk with death, and T. wears a bib of death blood, and S. has spit up his last words, and W. is dead in his own shit, and it is too late to stop things. Try putting down that fried chicken leg when the rest of the bird has flown away from you. The virgins, are they loving you now, S.? Have they smelled your pomade and licked your teeth? T., do they make you do paradisal housework? Fluff the clouds? W., are you incontinent in paradise?

Right now, the passengers are under my control. I know. They know. No one else can fly the fucking plane. Except I can't fly it either. For the 358th time, I check the autopilot functions. All systems assure me that I control my fate. My senses assure me that fate is bound by another's strings.

M. makes a noise that sounds like "piss-shit."

The stewardess, the unplump one, sashays into the cockpit.

"I am too tired to be cruel to you," I say, "but did I summon you?"

She says, "Look, jerkface," and then she points her long calloused finger.

I see it now: It's the end. Off in the far fat American blue sky, it's some kind of fighter jet. It's two fighter jets. It's three. It's four. They fly in robust balletic arcs. They literally swoop. It's beautiful in the way the mouse thinks that about the hawk.

I say, "Don't worry. They'll never shoot us down."

She says, "I gave up worrying six hours ago. That's your bullshit now."

The jets fly up and around. They are elegant and precise. I feel that the pilots might possibly be looking in at me, at M. with his vomit necktie. What would they see in the ashtray of my soul?

As the jets whoosh around our fragile 747, they make an exclamation of power and noise. Their rumble shakes the entire sky. They surround us, fly with us, one above, one below, one on each side. I hear the radio make its dead fizz. It was M.'s idea to rip it out, castrate its wires. These jet fighters would like to talk to me, call me names, slap my face, attach a dog's collar to my pimpled neck, but the radio refuses to speak, and I sit at the controls, which allow me to control nothing.

Black Box, I've read my own mind. It's a book full of typos.

Black Box, I'm an infidel.

Black Box, I smoked marijuana. I took Xanax. I lusted after tits and hot tubs.

Black Box, I am telling you this because you are the holder of secrets.

The sky spills out before the cockpit like a tangle of delicate blues. It's hard to believe this sky can break open and that all sorts of shit— acid rain, satellites, meteors—can fall out of it. Today the sky is at peace with itself. I cut across it, dog-paddle through it, wear the sky like a bath towel. I wrap the sky around my waist. I grab at the cloudy sponges. I enjoy my perch on the bathtub of heaven.

I don't care about those fighter jets.

And then the unplump stewardess bangs her hand against my shoulder.

"Mr. Killer, sir," she says. "There's also a problem with the toilets. We need you to fix it, Mr. Terrorist."

Her fear of me has shrunk in inverse proportion to my fear of her. She keeps the passengers at bay. She delivers icy drinks. She knows how to open the various hatches. She has calloused hands like a man and little feet and a long nose that she twitches when you don't answer her questions. Her nose wiggles me into submission.

She has a brown eye and a blue eye. I point this out to her, by way of small talk, and she says, "Friggin' colored contacts," and she messes with her left eye, and then she looks at me with two matching eyes, dirty brown clouded with red.

"Better?" she asks.

Her nose begins its awful jitters.

"Quite better, ma'am."

The fighter jets ring us. One seems to wave its wings at us.

"They will shoot us down," I say.

"I friggin' wish," she says.

I am no longer a potential martyr. I am the one everyone will blame.

"Tell the passengers we will jettison all bodily waste," I say. "How many sodas, beers, packets of pretzels do we have left?"

She says, "The same as when we left. We never run out."

I say, "Another beverage service then," and shoo her out of the cockpit.

Black Box, I no longer have the luxury of feelings. I couldn't love the unplump one even if she allowed me to. Emotions have been banned from my head. I think of my brother, and I think of nothing. I think of my good old dead friend W., and I think of nothing. W., I kicked your ass at John Madden Football, and then I pumped my fist. W., your eyes said you were lonely. Your eyes said ask me about my mother. Your eyes said you would always bite on the flea-flicker.

Black Box, I would never under any circumstances challenge you to John Madden Football. This is the promise I make. Gods cheat. I know this. You would pretend to bite on the flea-flicker, but then you would show your real unbroken teeth. Black Box, I feel I can be frank with you.

What you do is what you do, and at the end of the day that is all you have. Roll up the prayer rug, if you still pray, and turn on the cable. The day is over and you have sinned and destroyed or maybe taken a nice walk down to the park, swallowed a bottled beer, whizzed behind a tree, peeked out at pretty women displaying the tops of their breasts in all manners of fabrics designed to entice and repel stains.

Formerly One Blue Eye comes into the cockpit.

"Senator Terror, may I have a word with you? There's a passenger who wants to say a few words."

I say, "Just a few."

"Yes, sir," she says. "Your wish is my command, Master of Disaster."

America is the wealthiest country in terms of sarcasm and eyeliner.

A tall angular man with thick glasses and greasy gray hair enters the cockpit. He wears a T-shirt and waves his dirty white dress shirt as if it were a flag. He makes an effort to appear meek.

He says, "We beg for your mercy."

It is the bloody-voiced man, the one who pleads for the lord.

I say, "You have my mercy."

He wipes his eyeglasses with the tail of his dirty white surrender shirt.

He has a long hooked nose and tiny black bird eyes. M. gasps and groans as if he is wrestling a coma.

This bloody-mouthed Bird Eye looks at us, almost sneers buts swallows it back, and all I can think is: We have the ability to wipe out skylines, smash your horizons, make you stay home, huddled by the teapot, using bottled water, fearing our arsenic from the tap. Stay at home, drink your herbal fear, stew in the dregs of disaster. We are strong and brave and self-destructive. We explode in your living rooms, up in your heads. I think this, but I am so tired.

I say it again. "You have my mercy."

He says, "We need to land this plane. There are children and women."

I say, "You have my mercy, but there are things I can't control."

He says, "You, too, have my mercy. I could kill you right here with my hands and my teeth."

I show him the hard black plastic of the air marshal's gun.

His voice gets higher, gets bloody again, says, "You, too, have my mercy."

As he leaves the cockpit, he doesn't wave his surrender shirt.

Black Box, what does mercy mean?

Nothing changes on the plane except minds and fears and bodies. My own smells have become fierce and thick, the scent of a turkey leg dipped in a swamp. The deodorant surrendered over Chicago. The plane keeps going; the Cokes never stop; the peanuts never run out. Biology and chemistry don't stop either. I need a shave and a bath, and for the last twelve hours I have been squeezing up my sphincter.

M. snuffles in his sleep, occasionally wakes and screeches in a dream language.

I am beginning to understand him.

He howls, "Kikikikikiki."

"Yes," I say, "that is correct."

Finally we have a mutual understanding.

M. yells, "Glaaaah."

I say, "Surely, you're understating things."

We no longer have a failure to communicate. I almost miss the wall of sneers and obscenity and huffy snorts that once stood between us.

M. spills a puddle of greasy-looking green liquid out of his mouth onto the floor.

I say, "Someone needs a hug."

M. yells, "Flahhhh."

I say, "Indubitably."

The new growth of my beard scrapes my hand. I had hoped it would come back after the mission. I had pictured the hair poking out of my ashes. Without it, I look like a child.

I summon the stewardess.

"Hello, Doctor Death."

Her words don't even bruise. They tickle and irritate.

"I need more coffee. I need a wakeup call."

Formerly One Blue Eye slaps her palm down on my head, and something—a ring she wears?—sends a clanging down deep, through my skull, all through my body. It settles in my shoes, where my toes writhe. She would not have done this if I were taller, paler, handsomer, crueler.

She says, "You have another friend who would like to speak with you."

"Not now," I say. "I am flying the plane."

Which is a lie, albeit a convincing one. The needles stay fiercely still. The plane still drinks from a full canteen of fuel. The jets to either side thrum powerfully.

Black Box, I fear you're not listening to me.

Black Box, I wear a coat of secrets. The secrets are warm, comfortable, worn, not frayed. They bend to my body and my will. Black Box, I am naked before you. I tried to scuttle the mission. It came to me as a spritz of brain juice: If we miss the plane, we cannot destroy it. Black Box, as I drove to the airport, I took several wrong turns. I lefted when I should have righted. I disregarded M.'s smashing fist as it encouraged my shoulder to make correct turns.

Of course, Black Box, you know as well as I: The plane, your plane, this plane, also was delayed. We were late; it was later. We made our way toward the giant steel vulture. Security pressed its eyes into our own, into our skin, into our passports. They are careful fakes, our names, our passports, our stories. Black Box, I will tell you my passport name: Jonathan Wayne. But you, Black Box, may call me A., which as M. liked to say, "could stand for asshole."

The passengers roar into cell phones. I can hear them, all those voices. Their fear of me is gone. My fear of me continues. They are the voices from the clouds, and they do not sing. They call their loved ones, various police and government agencies. Mostly they murmur. Only the bloody-voiced man is fully audible, and he is talking to his lawyer.

We sail over Nebraska or perhaps Idaho. It's a long fucking country, and I've lost track. It goes like this: Probably cornfield, probably cornfield, possibly cornfield, perhaps alfalfa field, probably cornfield. The green circles of field stare up at me; they never blink.

A man dressed in a black woolen suit barges into the cockpit, looks at M., who snores and leaks spittle.

I say, "Beauty rest."

The man pushes out his fat little hand, says, "I am Albert T. Wellington. Seat 3B. First class."

I say, "I am flying the plane."

This 3B has curls of worried blondish hair. He looks at his notes, scribbled on the back of the in-flight magazine.

He says, "We suggest that rations be limited to two drinks, two granola bars, and one bag of peanuts in coach. Double rations in first class."

I say, "But things, the food, the drinks, they never run out."

"Yet," he says. "Not yet."

He shakes his dry-mop skull.

"Not yet," he says.

I dismiss him by showing the handle of the air marshal's gun. I can hear the whisperings behind the cockpit door, which I latch and bolt and double-check. I can hear the rhythm of knuckles against the steel, but it can withstand pistol shots and battering rams; we did copious research; I know these things.

I fly my plane. My plane flies me.

Black Box, we must breathe deeply from the plasticky recycled air. It churns for us, and down below, life swarms with green things, glorious plantlike objects. How can we tell what's growing from up here? We can't. I imagine fresh green rows of artificial replacement kidneys and Reeboks, satellite dishes and video games. The land of plenty offers up everything, including jet fighters above and below and to the sides.

Black Box, I would like to slink back to a cramped coach seat, slump against the pillow, watch the movie, slip into the crowd. I will be polite to my fellow passengers. I won't tip my seat back into the personal space of the being behind me. I will withhold my smells until I get to the restroom.

Black Box, when I went to the training camp with my older brother in 1998, I was sixteen years old. So long ago. I remember the sweat and the dust clogging my nostrils and the riddle of always being thirsty. I was the weakest soldier. I never cried at night. I scored the highest on the intelligence test.

My brother was a tall pretty man with beliefs in his head. He died in a field near Shanksville, Pennsylvania.

On the day he died, M. said to me, "I'm your brother now."

Nine years and two months later, brother M. appears to be choking, and I listen to this carefully. There's a message there, except it's running out of oxygen.

M. with his fat mustache and his hair goop.

"It's styling gel," he once said to me.

The virgins of paradise will love his styling products and his Taco Bell breath. The vomit needs help. I wrap my fingers around his neck. His skin is soft, but the tissue beneath feels tough and bony. I squeeze and press my fingers into him. He emits a high hollow moan. I press. Press. Flex fingers. M. no longer seems much of a threat. Harder. Harder. My thumbs cramp up, but some missions can't be aborted. Hate has its own momentum. I hold this grip, and the blood throbs in my arms, and I bite my own lips, and I close my own eyes, and I ignore the shakes burrowing in my fingers and wrists, and I count to 117.

Black Box, at some point in every life, the moaning stops.

Black Box, I would like to try a similar maneuver on myself, put you in charge. Except all you do is listen, wait, judge, brood, whirr. You are in here somewhere. You are everywhere. You can't help now.

Black Box, your mother was a Ford Fairmont. Your mother wears snow tires. She leaks oil. Your father was a gas pump. Your mother got around. She liked the nozzle if you know what I mean. Black Box, am I getting too personal? Can't we get along?

This plane will not obey the laws of physics, of supply and demand, of consumption, of god. It is a willfully obstinate and unruly creature. My fingers clutch the lying throttle. The instruments fib. Everything offers a false promise. Black Box, only you are solid.

I wait for the sun to go down, and it refuses. The day stretches out forever, seared into existence. We need a philosopher of time. We need to think things through.

M. says, "Waaaal."

Except he is dead, and he says nothing.

Each night we devoured hate. Hate with beans. Macaroni and hate. M. served it up. These American dogmen, he said, they deserve to die smelling their own asses. Hate on toast.

They will kill us, our ways, our god. Their McDonald's will starve us.

The American pigeons must be plucked and roasted.

Hate salad.

Black Box, I will tell you how to mix up hate, serve it on your best china.

Except I forget all the recipes. I am sleepy and forgetful. M. is the Chef Boyardee, and he cooks in paradise.

The country remains where it is, far below and unreachable.

The fighter planes remain brash and loud, fiery and swift. They practically brush against my craft. I assume they are trying to talk to me. My broken radio won't let them in. They have no idea what is happening here, and in that way, they are like me.

I want to tell them they should cherish this moment. Press pause. As long as we stay up here nothing gets destroyed. Keep your thoughts high and mighty.

Waiting is purgatory. And boredom is purgatory. And the mosquito in the tent is purgatory. And the instant before the Milky Way does or does not drop out of the candy machine is purgatory. Purgatory is all I can imagine. And the thing is I shouldn't even believe in such a thing. But I do. I see it everywhere.

I miss my flight simulator and my FM 98.3 and my John Madden Football. Black Box, I would go long and deep on you, even on first and ten.

My face feels like a bowl of oatmeal, and my brain's part of that goo. When I squint, the sky adds black, blinks from blue to purple. I try to imagine the denim sky on fire, but even my mind lacks that much lighter fluid.

Several new fighter jets scar my view of air and space. They make loud, graceful, threatening rushes. They possess a thundering menace, and they appear to be gathering before me. If there are voices in the clouds, they are lost to the groans of machinery. I will have to sing the songs on my own.

The jet fighters are massed nine hundred yards away in the smoke of the clouds, and they make me forget all the words. Eight hundred yards. Black Box, they are coming.

Hatred keeps you lean and grinning. But I am so full. I feel sorry for everyone. The jet pilot who must commit the next crime. The fat stewardess and her damp face. The air marshal, whom I stabbed in the neck with a ballpoint pen. He had already killed people. We had already killed people. At a certain point it seems fair on both sides of the ledger, and I'd like to land down there in that little green field. From here, it is a slick lush green, like a chili pepper. The passengers could chase me across it, all the way across that chili pepper, and I could run as fast as possible, as fast as a child, and still they could catch me, and I could bite the earth, and say, "It isn't a chili pepper. It's fucking grass." All this, of course, is conjecture.

Black Box, why do I tell you this? Because you and only you will outlast us.

There's no going back. I cannot turn. I cannot turn. The future swallows me up, and I cannot turn from it.

THE DIRTY BOY

AUTHOR'S NOTE: *Although for the sake of verisimilitude I consulted www.thedirtyboy.com and Paco Winks's excellent* The Dirty Boy of Athens, Georgia *(2006), the following story is a product of my imagination.*

THEY TELL THE STORY to scare freshmen: There's a guy who lives in a park downtown, and he doesn't bathe, and he's covered with filth, and he's really, really famous, and he's so gross it messes with people's minds.

You don't believe them.

You could have stayed home at BU or even Tufts (your SAT scores were that good, and you ran cross-country, and you did public service senior year, picking up aluminum cans that fuckheads threw from their pukemobiles onto the side of the highway, and you even wrote six poems that were published in the student literary magazine), but somehow you ended up at the University of Georgia, and you aren't going to believe these hick stories about smelly homeless guys who don't wash their hands.

Then you see him from a distance. You Google him, and he gets 820 hits. You believe.

He's dirt, covered with grit, covered with mud, and he's just across from you in the park. He's eating an ice cream cone, perhaps vanilla, and all that white is dissolving into the living mud of his face.

He's either an old boy or a young man. He looks like an ashtray. He looks like a coal miner. He looks like a fireman after the flames. He looks like a golem. He looks like muck. He's not wearing a shirt, and ropy muscles undulate under his acquired blackness. His hair is a helmet of grease. His nose, you don't even want to think about that nose.

He throws the cone into a trash can, and then he slinks away.

You peer into the can. The cone sits there next to a banana peel and a used condom tied shut with a square knot. You reach in and pull it out. There are five dots of black grime, his prehistoric fingerprints, on the waffled brown, and you make a note of this: The Dirty Boy eats sugar cones—and then you sniff—and French vanilla.

Back in your dorm room, you Google him again. "The Dirty Boy" gets 6,539 hits.

Your roommate, M. Givens, never shows up. You'll never even find out what the fucking M. stands for.

All you know is that M. Givens allegedly lives in La Grange, Georgia, which is not even a dot on the map of your mind.

You could make up crazy fucking names starting with the letter M. You could. You have the capabilities.

Martha, Miriam, motherfucker!

But you don't have time for that bullshit.

You rub sleep from your eyes and slurp from the bottle of mouthwash.

You pull up your T-shirt and examine yourself in the bathroom mirror. You imagine greasy fingerprints on your skin, then spit your mouthful of medicine-brine into the sink. Your tongue burns from the purity of it.

You decide to stop shaving your armpits.

Do you have an edge? Of course you have an edge. The world has edges.

Of course you punched people at Deerfield Academy.

Of course you got expelled.

Of course you forged the check.

Of course you keyed Gabriela's Jeep.

Of course you flipped out on people.

Of course you took acid.

And speed.

And Oxycontin.

Of course it was fun.

Of course your parents are sick of you. You're sick of you, too.

You buy two hundred and fifty-seven dollars worth of textbooks and spread them out on the unused bed.

The books stare at you; you stare back; the books stare harder. They are impenetrable, expensive, possibly radioactive.

Your dorm room never gets too hot or too cool, and this equanimity tends to piss you off, which makes you summon your demons through the usual channels.

Your parents cluck through the phone.

You say, "Everything at the cafeteria tastes like mashed potatoes, except the mashed potatoes."

You don't ask if you can come home. Your parents don't offer.

They're having the house painted.

You say, "Let me guess—beige."

Your mother says, "Smoked Oyster."

You picture a blackened mussel flaccid in its shell.

You don't like the male RA, and you don't like the female RA. You don't like the coed bathrooms. You don't want anyone in there with you when you do your business, when you tend to your earwax, when you floss.

There are ways to get people to leave you alone. You've mastered the eerie silence. You don't even nod at these fucking people.

You can't help it. His grossness is magnificent.

He possesses a geological aura of stink and grime.

His pants might have been green in a previous life. His shirt is grease. Sometimes he juggles with rocks, and sometimes he scrapes little chips of filth off his body. The muscles in his chest twitch rhythmically—you know he does this on purpose. From a certain distance, he's the shadow of a clean and proper being.

You get up close. That dirt is thick. There are layers and layers, and he smells like several different people, like a rotten kumquat, like moldy french fries and warm loam and used toilet paper and hot red pepper. The Dirty Boy makes you sneeze.

He says, "America, I've given you all, and now I'm nothing," and then he goes on and on like this: "America, I've stomped on your cell phone. America, I've given you Yodels and those peanut-butter thingies. You know, Funny Bones. America, I schtup with a bear in the woods. America, when will you play the glockenspiel?"

You like the steady, fucked-up words coming out of his shit-brown lips.

He's a fucking poet of the earth, and he's detached and shielded with grime, and once, in the middle of the day, you see him pull out the dirt-black nub of his penis to piss on a bush.

You look away, then back, then away, then back, and then he is done, spent, zippered.

He has a digital camcorder, and he films all this shit.

He gets interviewed by members of the local press.

He gets ticketed for disturbing the peace.

He gets little bags of marijuana from the hipsters.

Rubbing his belly is rumored to bring all varieties of goodish luck—small lottery winnings, favorable divorce settlements, disease-free gynecological exams—and UGA alums pay him in excess of twenty dollars for this indulgence.

You watch these transactions: the belly rubbing (he moans lasciviously), the ritual cleansing of hands with Purell.

You Google him, and he gets 83,547 hits. He's well-known in several foreign countries. The French fucking love him. He has fan clubs. His own Web site is updated every night. You can make a contribution via PayPal.

You send him thirteen cents.

You look for trouble. Trouble looks for you.

You and trouble meet up on the corner of Fifth and Whatever-the-fuck-street-it-is, where the wind could rattle the maracas of your soul, if there were any wind and if you had any soul.

Trouble wants you to fuck up The Dirty Boy.

You're already fucked up yourself. It's the blank part of the morning that still thinks it's the night, and you have vodka in your belly, motor oil in your veins. It couldn't be blood. It couldn't be motor oil. It's dirt.

You have mud in your veins, and you search and you search and you search, and you sniff at the hot still Georgia air with all the ratness of your being.

You need the tickle and thrum of the wind, but you can't smell a damn thing except your own musty armpits, which remind you of Velveeta.

You wake up in the park.

The sun spits cancer upon you.

You type "The Dirty Boy" into Google, and you get 157,391 hits.

On MySpace, he has 5,998 friends.

You say, "You should've paid for me to go to Tufts."

Your parents' telephoned voices take turns ladling out random words, a stew of disconnection.

The Smoked Oyster wasn't subtle enough.

Your mother patiently describes three shades of off-white.

They're getting new carpeting, too.

The drinking is easy. It's the no-longer-drinking that's hard.

You run all the way across campus, past that arch UGA people are so proud of, past all that marble, past all those old bricks. Everything appears and disappears: drunk people, smoked sausages, salad tongs, Handi Wipes. You reduce it all, the world, to specks in your eye—there, now gone.

You don't stop running until you're curled in blankets. Lights out. Eyes stoppered. Bed spinning. Mind fucked.

Your brain is working again. Perhaps. You feel a twinge in your right temple like the pulse of a creature that will spring fully formed from your head. Not a goddess. It's a mangy chipmunk with an overbite. And bad breath. It doesn't like it inside your brain.

You try to drown it with water, with milk, with Mountain Dew, but the chipmunk floats to the top of your skull, where it chews and chews.

The Dirty Boy technically signifies more than dirt. He could be The Body Odor Boy or The Pariah Boy or The Festering Sore Boy.

Plus, he's more like a man.

He gets around these days. He's been on "Springer," where he received a case of Ivory Soap and a kick in the nuts. He's been called an abomination by several state senators. Oprah wants no part of him. He had that cable-access show for a while, where he would mumble into the camera for twenty-seven and a half minutes. Nothing he said meant more than nothing. That was its glory. The footage doesn't lie.

If his show were still on, you would watch it every week. You would mumble along. You would sing the theme song, which contains several variations of the word fuck, gerunds, transitive verbs, mixed metaphors dealing with mothers and the people who love them.

Class is where you go when you get bored of your dorm room, the park, and the library archives where they keep The Dirty Boy files.

Class creates a nice change in your schedule. You discover that your comp TA has treacherous nose hair, and your political science professor flaps his arms around as if he were a duck taking flight from a pond of armpit sweat. In history, you confirm that people have always been filthy. The present is simply the past coated with deodorant.

In the archives, you meet three graduate students—two from American studies and one from sociology—and all three are writing doctoral dissertations on The Dirty Boy. You explain your own dissertation, your hunger to know the truth, the bacteria, the flesh.

"It's not the dirt that's important," you say, and they nod knowingly.

You explain that you're a super genius, that you attended Columbia at nine. You explain that Tufts wanted to give you a full ride. They nod knowingly. You use the term "hegemony of cleanliness" at random times. They ask you for advice.

"Can you imagine being him?" the sociologist asks.

He's the talker among you, and he smells of Skittle breath. He's unable or perhaps unwilling to squeeze the dour blackheads on the tip of his nose.

You say, "I'm overripe if I skip just one fucking shower."

"Same here," he says.

You try to imagine. You try to summon up the imaginary filth. You try and try, but the dirt of your mind won't stick to your skin.

You are not him.

Sometimes you're barely you.

He makes fewer and fewer public appearances. Mainly you and the grad students watch his offerings on YouTube. He doesn't look so dirty anymore, especially as you watch him on the computer monitor. The sociologist believes the dirt has been washed away and replaced with the smearing of burnt cork. Or perhaps some kind of cosmetic.

"He's getting a little too *you know*," one of the American studies dudes says.

You all nod and watch the digital recordings.

The Dirty Boy smells like a whirring hard drive.

The archives are deep in the basement of the library, the irritating bowels, where the dust smells like something alive, except just barely.

The graduate students take you out for pizza and ply you with pitchers of beer. It's possible that they want to get into your pants.

All four of you smell like yeast and the yellow tang of old newspaper clippings.

The graduate students fail miserably at karaoke. You sing "I Will Survive" to rousing, possibly heartfelt cheers.

Your brain feels pinched in its bony cage.

The key is to keep on going. You can do it. You will stay drunk forever and lie in the park, and the dirt will come and the rain will come and the dust will come and the smut will grow on your face, and you, too, will be pure.

The Dirty Boy sells his own artwork on e-Bay. When you ask Google for its insight, "The Dirty Boy" delivers 298,763 hits.

Your dorm room feels too small and also vacant.

You imagine M. Givens knocked up and working at the La Grange Wal-Mart. You imagine M. Givens in bed awaiting a liver transplant. You imagine M. Givens on the crew team at Tufts.

On his Web site, The Dirty Boy announces the public cleansing. He needs a better publicist, a better editor:

On October 26 outside Sanford Stadium, I will wash
away 2 years of grime. That's 740 days of filth and vermin.
Of lice and a toe that I nearly lost to gangegreen.

This is the end of The Dirty Boy as we know it. I will
enter a new faze of being.

This show is intended for mature audiences.

The sociologist makes a sound like a whisk and says, "Gangrene? Have we verified gangrene?"

The Dirty Boy shouts, "Is everybody ready for a party?"

He's wearing a green smock that looks vaguely like a graduation gown.

Then he says he'll only do it, get truly clean, if people pass the hat and collect $3,000. He sounds a little whiny.

"Sellout," says the sociologist.

Three local radio stations are there and the FOX affiliate from Atlanta. Someone says Tom Wolfe's in the crowd to write about it for *Rolling Stone*. None of you can spot the white suit.

Mainly it's frat boys, drunks, old men smoking tiny cigars, and the occasional inappropriately dressed woman.

You say, "There must be two thousand people here."

And one of the American studies guys says, "Three thousand."

The other says, "That's a buck each."

When the hat comes to you, it's surprisingly clean.

"It's a Biltmore beaver," says the sociologist.

It's a size 7, and you each put in a dollar.

Mostly he's a deep dark stench of a color, too brown to be black.

His teeth are a Post-It yellow. Looking at him tastes like pickles and cocaine and the Dead Sea.

The great dark smell of him hums in your ears.

During the entire hat-passing, The Dirty Boy does calisthenics, push-ups, some weird type of yoga.

You thought it might be more official, serious-like.

Then two women in bikinis simply spray him with a hose. He uses Irish Spring soap. There's a large Hollywood-style camera and a towel that says Irish Spring.

The sudsing lasts fifteen minutes.

He's wearing a little G-string with a shamrock on it.

He's irredeemably alabaster, and his hair—surprise—is dirty blond.

He looks deflated, smaller, ferret-like.

His teeth remain disgusting, but still.

The sociologist says, "I shower longer than that on a daily basis."

You and the grad students get pizza and beer, but there is no karaoke in your soul.

Someone has ruined everything. Your parents. The financial aid people. The grad students. M. Givens. The Dirty Boy.

The archives fill you with the sickness unto death.

The American studies grad students drop out of school, and the sociologist obsessively rewrites his opening chapter. He sits in the archives and chews on a pencil.

When he sees you, he says, "The dirt's still out there."

They say he's hiding, acquiring new layers of oily crust.

Some day soon he will rise triumphant. He will smell like the dying goo of a garbage can.

"That ain't gonna happen," you say.

How do you know?

You just do. You just know.

You have nothing fucking better to do than go to class.

Honestly, you don't even Google him anymore.

The commercial comes on once, and you switch the fucking channel.

You start to get Cs and sometimes even Bs. You acquire friends and hookups. You get drunk only on weekends.

In your Introduction to Fiction class, you read "How to Become a Writer" by Lorrie Moore and "How to Date a Browngirl, Blackgirl, Whitegirl, or Halfie" by Junot Diaz. You don't buy any of it.

Someone says, "How can that you be me?"

"Exactly," you say.

But your mind, that splendid bundle of nerves and gigabytes, plays tricks, switches the channel, the perspective.

Now you can see yourself coated with mud, see the hair from your pits hanging like dreadlocks, see the gruesome stares. You can feel the sludge on your skin. The germs want your pores and all of your crevasses.

The dirt would be a crust, and you would lose yourself inside it. Your skin would ooze, your hair would itch, and your nose would never forgive. It would be like wearing a suit made of bugs, of leeches, of the smallest germs, the kind that are so teensy and so deadly they're nuclear.

You imagine the Web cam, the paparazzi, the reality show.

An itch frolics on your palm, your suddenly feral palms.

You go into the bathroom. You let the water run until it offers some heat. You pummel the soap a bit. You get a good lather going. You scrub.

At a frat party someone says, "It's hard being dirty."

And you say, "Baby, it's hard on everyone."

THIS DOCUMENT SHOULD BE RETAINED
AS EVIDENCE OF YOUR JOURNEY

PATTERSON PULLED ON bleach-stained khakis, glared at his sleeping wife, tucked frustration into his waistband along with the tail of his shirt, and glared again. He helped lots of kids, troubled or not, but that didn't mean he liked them sleeping in his house.

"I'm awake," Vicki said. "I feel you looking at me."

"Love," he said, "I'm going to wake that kid good and up."

The stranger was one of those fucked-up white kids, one of those suburban druggies who made Patterson reconfigure infertility as a kind of blessing. Vicki's cousin's kid, a once-removed type or some other questionable and ill-defined relation. He was seventeen and asleep on Patterson's couch.

First, Patterson shook a woolly shoulder, and then, after the kid—fully dressed and pre-dirtied—stood up, stretched, and slipped into a grimace, Patterson shook his hand.

"I'm Patterson. Jim Patterson, but Patterson's fine, not Mister or any of that shit."

The grimace looked back at him, said, "I'm Jacey."

Jacey looked as if he were knotted together with twine. Born to slouch. He had a gristly pimply face and floppy blond hair that fell across bloodshot eyes. Patterson brought the kid into the kitchen, where Vicki was making things work. She placed a bowl in front of Patterson.

"Be careful," she said. "It's hot."

"Hot hot or spicy hot?" Patterson asked.

"It's oatmeal," she said.

The kid refused sustenance, watched Patterson eat.

"Hunger strike," Patterson said. "It's not going to work."

The oatmeal boxed Patterson's ears, and the coffee cheered him. On the way out the door, he grabbed the hammer he had left in the bathroom, found a mysterious gentle hum rising from his throat, told the kid to get moving.

"Shut up, my love," he said to Vicki as he sealed her lips with his own. He pinched her ass through a minimum of three pajama-like layers. He felt the ghost of the springiness that had been her young flesh.

"You think you're some young fresh buck," she said.

He did think as much, and the kid said, "She's still pretty," and Patterson said, "You keep your mouth shut and let me drive."

Patterson didn't mind the drive. It allowed him to build a Detroit of his mind. His brain glazed windows and repaired potholes. His brain bulldozed collapsing buildings, sucked up the trash, killed all the seagulls.

Back when he was a boy, his parents left Detroit the way everyone left it: gladly. Now he kept coming back. Patterson owned eighteen apartment buildings, right in the city, Cass Corridor, not the worst area, not the best. Mostly he rented to People of Color, and he capitalized this in his head. A softy 1980s term, made him think of purple folks and tangerine ones, but he used it too sometimes.

They were his people, and this was his journey: Six days a week, sometimes seven, he drove the twenty-five minutes down I-75 to fix toilets, patch drywall, flush rats from basements.

He got his rent checks in the mail, tried not to think of the city as rot and rust and garbage, left folks alone. He hired the kids in his buildings, though, lots of them. He liked the kids. They had not yet fucked up their lives, and Patterson handed out a few sly dollars here and there, to scrub the odd floor, to scrape the sooty paint off a tired wall. He paid up front, smiled, and said "thanks," "good job," "what about a 'you're welcome,'" "say hi to your mom," "behave yourself," "take care of yourself," "stay in school," "how's your dad," "keep that yelling down," "don't you end up like those guys out there," "if you need help you just ask."

This Jacey had been foisted on him, but he was a worker. Patterson had him hosing down a bathroom, bleaching it back to as close as it could get to new.

At noon, Patterson went out to get them meatball sandwiches and Cokes, down the block and up past the place where the hookers hung their lips out like nooses.

"Let me suck your dick," one of them said in a way that made it unclear who would be doing a favor for whom.

"Do I look like I need to pay for any dick sucking?" Patterson asked. "No, stop. Don't answer that."

She was the skinny dried-out one, the oldest teenager he had ever seen. He kept his feet moving the way he kept his money in his pocket, his dick in his pants. Around here, a bill turns into crack faster than it can turn into quarters.

Patterson pushed his feet into a trot. When he came back the kid would be stalling, plotzing around, pressing his face up against a window. Patterson would sneak into the apartment and throw a spark into him.

The kid was in up to his elbows in the toilet bowl.

"Wash up, and we'll do some fucking eating," Patterson said.

In the afternoon they painted, Patterson with the roller, the kid cutting in the corners with a brush.

"You should have a radio," Jacey said. "I like DMX and D-12, Jay-Z. I like Eminem *and* Insane Clown Posse. I was in that Kid Rock video, the one they just shot. I like all that. The usual stuff. Mainly I just hang out with my niggaz."

The kid was pale and loud and frail, and he positioned the bill of his baseball cap at a careful and ludicrous angle. Patterson whittled Jacey down with his eyes. A child.

"You watch your fucking mouth," Patterson said.

Jacey went to NA, started living with some friends in the city, worked with Patterson three days a week.

Jacey worked hard, sure, but he was a talker. Blah, blah, blah. Pistons, crack whore, Eminem. The kid's mouth was a leaky faucet, and the MTV bullshit just dripped out of it.

Each morning Patterson said, "I pick what we listen to, and if you don't likey-like, don't listen."

And each day at some point, the kid tuned in some rap-type shit on the radio, Patterson's radio.

Man, the kid pissed him off.

Jacey just couldn't leave anything alone.

That time they cleaned up the alley, three little black kids, maybe preschoolers, were taking crazy looping shots at a basketball hoop. It was forty fucking degrees, and none of them wore a coat. Patterson and Jacey watched, hooted after a good play.

One of the kids was smaller than the ball, and he had to dribble with both hands. Didn't matter. These kids laughed and chattered, and one of them said, "There's Mr. Patterson," and it was a happy coincidence when the ball went through the hoop.

Just watching them made Patterson feel like a crisp fall apple, still juicy with life. The cold didn't stop these kids. They didn't care that the ball was half flat and balding.

Just watching them was enough. But Jacey had to join in, take some three-pointers, high-five the kids.

"Man," Jacey said, "they're cool little niggaz."

Patterson's apple turned to mush.

He told Jacey to shut his piehole, fuck off for the afternoon. Patterson gave each of the little kids a five-dollar bill.

"This is money I'm not paying you today," he said to Jacey.

That night at dinner, Vicki ladled stew into Patterson's bowl, and Patterson ladled it into his mouth with a crust of bread.

"That Jacey," he said. "Every other word is nigger-this, nigger-that. Any angle you look at him, he's 100 percent fuck-up."

The skin around Vicki's eyes crinkled. Patterson didn't like what that meant, but he liked the way it looked. He liked her long fingers, too, even the way she scratched. Right then and there, she was reaching out and tugging on a tuft of short gray hair above his left ear. Yanking really.

"Around here," she said, "we take care of our people, no matter how they behave."

Alone in the house, Patterson let the answering machine click to life and pick up the call. "Patterson. Are you there? Patterson? Vicki? Will you pick up the phone? It's me, Jacey. I'm sort of stuck here, downtown, at, like, the bus station, at the big one, where the Greyhounds stop. I need some help. I don't have any money . . . "

Patterson heard a shuffling of wispy noises in the background. Maybe Jacey was talking to someone else, holding the phone away, muffling the receiver with a dirty shirtsleeve. Then Jacey was talking again.

"I really need a ride, and I don't have anyone to call. Except, I guess, you. I'll be here. I'll be here for . . . " The machine decided that Jacey had said enough.

Patterson let this message play four times in succession, strained his ears during the silent part, heard nothing, heard no fear, heard a little need, heard a little hitch in the voice that sounded like a practical joke. He didn't even like the kid.

He was too old for this bullshit.

As he walked out to the garage, Patterson thought that if Jacey were there and in trouble the kid would learn a tidy little lesson. If Jacey weren't there, Patterson would have a lesson of his own.

Two weeks later, winter settled in and stretched itself out. Patterson pulled on his burnt-orange parka and took on the snow. He was ungloved and puffing. When his nose started to run, his fingers searched for a Kleenex, and all they found was an old boarding pass: Detroit to Miami, it said on the front, along with his name, the flight number, the boarding gate. On the back, it said: "This document should be retained as evidence of your journey." The wording made no fucking sense.

It was probably five or six years ago, when his parents were still alive. He had flown down to Miami, shed the parka for a slathering of sunscreen, visited them for a few days. They had left the suburbs behind the same way they had left Detroit. When green pastures beckon, you don't stay and fertilize the fucking parking lot.

They had traded Michigan for the old-people Florida fantasy: condominium gates, middle-class sunshine, Bingo games, sand in the shoes, skin-cancer fears. They covered themselves with hats and mint-smelling ointment and long-sleeved shirts and faded cotton-twill pants.

Patterson blew his nose on the boarding pass and crumpled it back into a pocket. Now, he and Vicki were the last of the Pattersons.

Jacey was *not* a Patterson. Vicki knew that, whether she'd admit it or not.

It was all bullshit anyway.

No matter where you go, you have some fresh new shit—falling out of the sky, falling out of your head—to shovel.

The snow seemed to muddy itself long before it hit the earth, and Patterson sped up, tried to keep pace with the clouds. Two weeks ago, on the way downtown to the bus station, Patterson had backed slowly out the driveway and puttered all the way down Maple Street before he said *fuck this* and headed back to the house. He erased the phone message, said nothing to Vicki. For all he knew that Jacey kid was still there.

If he liked the kid, sure, he would have picked him up. And if the kid had been a real relative, Patterson would have picked him up then, too. And if Patterson had been completely positive the kid wasn't fucked up on some kind of drugs—sure. And if the kid had been sick or injured, then too. And if the kid had been black, Patterson would have definitely picked him up.

Patterson told his mind to hush. He concentrated on shoveling snow, one of the last of the Manly Missions, like whittling, and burning acrid piles of spent tires, and gobbling up the fatty meat that wants to kill you.

Patterson scratched the brown-gray scrub of his naked head, and the shovel scraped against the tar of the driveway. Piles of white began to surround him.

From the house, Vicki yelled, "Don't overdo it." She waved, and then the futzy red door closed behind her.

That was the nicest thing she'd said to him in two weeks.

She knew about the kid. Somehow she knew. Every day, it was "Did Jacey show up today?" Or "Don't you think Jacey would've called by now?" Or "I wonder what Jacey's doing, right this very second."

Yes, Vicki knew. She had talked to her cousin. Or she had talked to Jacey. Or she had twirled her long fingers into Patterson's ears and picked out his thoughts as he slept.

Patterson spit on his hands, dug his boots into slippery traction. He got his arms pumping, felt his heart get a little flustered. Air puffed into his lungs and then bit like a rusty saw blade on the way out.

God. Scoop.

Damn. Dump.

White. Scoop.

Kids. Dump.

God. Scoop.

Damn. Dump.

Black. Scoop.

Kids. Dump.

He was in a rhythm now. Just scoop the snow and then dump it. That's how it goes, and then you repeat.

The bare skin of Patterson's hands blistered and surrendered a layer or two. Redness wept to the surface. In the snowbank, he buried all of his children.

THE COLLECTION

THOSE WERE THE DAYS when I mainly talked to myself.

"There's Betsy Ross's left-handed needle, Marion Barry's crack pipe, the hatchet George Washington didn't use when he didn't chop down that cherry tree."

The Collection was designed to astound and thrill, to astonish and free the mind. It was the morning after a dream. I wept for it.

"The collectors are coming," I said. "The collectors are coming."

They had been slavering for weeks, pranking Father, heckling, finding out if he still had Houdini's mittens.

Father was broke, spoiled, dried up tighter than a raisin. The collectors smelled bargains. They lurked in the bushes just beyond the electric fence.

We kept the best stuff—seventy of Barry Bonds's seventy-three home-run baseballs; that stained dress owned by that woman; Nixon's benign cyst, which looked suspiciously like a boiled peanut—locked in The Room of Wonder, where Father dozed and schemed in Archie Bunker's chair (liberated from the Smithsonian Institute in 1997).

"There's J. Edgar Hoover's corset, a bleeding pink. There's Henry Ford's lunchbox. There's Prince Albert's corpse nestled in its can."

The staff had been pink-slipped, terminated. Father and I stalked acres of empty house. A peopleless mansion attracts shadows and night-vision rodents. I heard them scuttling in the basement of my mind. The cars had been repossessed one by one. After the Camaro-Maserati-Porsche, I heard Father offer prayers and obscenities. He tried to get God or the GOP on the cell phone. Out on the grounds, the camellias choked, and the grass became a thick shag of weeds. The utilities officials alternated between wheedling and threatening. We sent checks, pen-stained fictions that kept the lights on.

We had played ping-pong with Clark Gable's paddle. We had raised the Titanic to cruise Bear Lake. We had worn cufflinks that bore a remarkable resemblance to Alexander Hamilton's missing knuckles.

The light of heaven poured through The Room of Wonder. That famous architect, the one with the shish-kabob name, he designed it.

"Bigger than a football field?" he asked.

Father said, "Bigger than two football fields."

And so it was said. And so it was built. The Room of Wonder had a skeletal dome of some New Age metal, a tragedy of glass. At midday it glinted and burned. Sunglasses were required. It made your retinas ache and itch.

I came under the hottest noon glow. No one else dared. I visited the stuff, and it spoke to me.

I resorted to metaphor.

"The Collection is America," I told Father. "It's America. Even the stuff you ripped off from other places."

"I am simply going to sell America for a while," he said. "And then we will buy a better one, a nicer, politer, cleaner America."

"Who wants to buy Canada?" I asked.

He didn't even pretend to respond. His ears were turned inward, listening to his cash-register brain, its empty till.

Every object told stories and something insidious: the truth. Father and I liked vintage hoochie girls, the scribblings of genius, stop-motion animation, the Founding Fathers' peccadilloes. We collected all this wonderful stuff. We hugged and squeezed it. It told us about our faults and our future, our dreams and our past, our small brilliancies and our splinted bones.

We had played catch with those baseballs. Father had wrapped himself in Liberace's robes. My personal noise had leaked out of Louis Armstrong's trumpet.

"There's the Liberty Bell, whole and glowing. We left the cracked one in Philadelphia. That's Woody Guthrie's first guitar. The inscription says, 'This Machine Kills Spiders.' He got it when he was six years old."

I said, "You don't want to sell Jimmy Hoffa's suicide note or that jar of William Taft fat."

"I don't want to sell them," Father said. "But I'm going to."

Father had lost his cash, his reverence for The Collection.

He seemed to operate under the continual assumption that something was on fire in an adjacent room. All day, I watched him sniff, then flee.

"Can't we get the Christie's people to do this?" I asked.

Father said, "The Christie's people didn't appreciate it when I told them to gargle with their own privates."

His eyelids slouched. He appraised The Collection through sharp little slits.

We established minimum bids for the Partridge Family bus, the Rosenbergs' erotica, the butterfly ballots.

And so it went. We appraised Benjamin Franklin's kite and electrified key.

It all had a price. I filled out the tags.

I understood the need. Didn't I know want?

Father's bubble went boom. All his dot-com bajillions disappeared into cyberspace, where they relaxed, played Pac-Man, and sent off spam. But Father hungered for another chance. He would turn The Collection back into money.

It made him drool and sweat.

He spent hours running his fingers through his hair. He was a great human tic, a wonderment of misgrooming. Over and over, he counted the thick wad of bills in his wallet. The bills were glorious and wrinkled. He made them himself with typing paper and a ballpoint pen.

Father summoned the collectors. I recognized their musty faces from the auctions in London, the secret galleries in New York, the black markets of Jakarta. Their hatred of us had boiled over, bubbled out of their mouths. We had purchased all the best things, and they despised our pastwealth, our us-ness, and they wanted the stuff, everything.

Except they didn't.

They came to insult and roar, point out cracks and blanch at our fingerprints.

The collectors sniffled and snuffed, hemmed without hawing. Mainly they frowned, grew bright shades of orange. We had ruined the stuff.

Artifacts should be pristine and polished, kept under glass, burglar-alarmed and locked away.

The one with the brown tassel mustache and the lazy eye, he fingered his herringbone pockets. He fumed and cursed.

"You cannot touch things and expect them to prosper," he said.

You can't pinch things, play with them, grab, squeeze, kiss with chapped lips. You can't taste things and bite them.

All these delicious things. Put them to use, and they're ruined.

Father stewed in a pruney bankrupt funk.

Father spent several minutes summoning the servants who no longer existed. Then he sighed. Perhaps he remembered his poverty, his impotence, his betrayal of The Collection. He emitted the yelp of a small dog wearing a cutesy little sweater in a rainstorm. He took to the streets. He posted signs. We would have a yard sale.

"What the collectors refused, the people will buy."

He said this over and over.

It began to make sense.

"That manuscript tells the story about The Muffin and The Scone, a trademarked fable purchased from Starbucks. That's Martha Washington's armor. There's Amelia Earhart's skeleton. That's Mark Twain's wooden leg."

Father said, "We're going to need a bigger cigar box than that."

He had two thousand dollars worth of change. The pennies alone were a hernia waiting to sprout.

The yard sale began.

The people came. They saw. They complained about prices.

No one could afford anything.

The people swarmed and buzzed. Hundreds of folks. They came in sagging pickups and on bicycles, in rust-speckled Mazdas and on bunioned feet.

The people trembled and gaped. They clustered like pimples. They doubted with their eyes, folded their hands into crackling fists. No one was too elegant or too happy. The prettiest woman owned the blackest eye. The prettiest man was running out of hair, smelled like a slouch. All of the children were so much closer to the dirt.

I begged them to touch, play with Frank Sinatra's bocce ball set, try on Mike Dukakis's army helmet.

Their watery eyes spoke strange and lonesome words.

The aptitude for pleasure had leached from their bones.

Eventually, the bold ones taught the meek.

They ran their fingers through Rapunzel's hair. They lit cigarettes with Sammy Davis Jr.'s lighter. Random fingers touched random hands grabbing hold of JFK's rosary.

A man with a face that looked sketched-in with pencil grabbed Knute Rockne's football and made a break for it. The general pillaging and hollering and bargaining began.

I encouraged this, actually.

I wanted people to steal it. Abscond with it. Perhaps I said these things out loud.

Children ran off with the various bones of Benedict Arnold. A gray-haired man smelling of books gave me sixteen cents for the Wright brothers' plane. A passel of Hells Angels said "please" and "no, no, no, after you" and in general supervised the looting.

A fat sexy woman bought the original Rubik's Cube carved out of wood. A little Asian girl bought Bettie Page's flannel nightgown. A man with a broken nose stuffed Dan Quayle's Mr. Potato Head deep into his pants.

I slashed the prices until they bled. I squoze them until they said uncle.
    I sold just about everything. I haggled myself down to the level where dollars don't exist. Father choked and rumbled, counted out pennies. He did all the math in his head, a geometry of wrinkles.

We obliterated it, sold everything for ninety-seven dollars. Father lost the money at the casino, came back, threatened me with anatomically impossible fates, and slept while weeping for three days.

The house mocked us. The empty refrigerator drooled and gaped. The plush carpet squished between our toes.
    Father and I camped out in The Room of Wonder. On the rare days when he spoke, some of his words were made entirely of spittle.

The dust motes flew uninhibited. The Room of Wonder glowed with dirt and a hollow-eyed sheen. I subsisted on the aches of hunger. Absence fed me. Without The Collection, I had nothing to talk about, except The Collection.
    Father didn't want to remember it in the proper way.

"Father," I asked, "what's a metaphor?"
    He gave me the finger.
    "Close enough," I said.

Father's tendons snapped as he flopped open his empty wallet. He did this often and noisily.

His hair abandoned him in clumps. He stuttered and refused to floss. We ate pork and beans cold out of the can.

When Father began the great warring dance, I was mesmerized and bewitched and horrified. Who knew he had rhythm? Who knew he could sprint and spring? Who knew he kept violence stuffed in his pockets where the change used to jingle?

He hollered and punched. The Room of Wonder, once just an idea after all, couldn't withstand fists, anger, destruction. The glass buckled, creaked, shattered. The sounds crackled through the air. Screeches. Sharp pebbles stuck in The Room of Wonder's craw. Father's fat-boned fists transformed the glass. He yelled and bled. The shards glimmered with crimson and sweat. He used his odd grace to lunge and destroy.

I ran from him, out of his shards, his words that shattered and cut and spattered.

I last saw him on MSNBC, CNN. He had corporate funding, government contracts, Hindenburgian plans, a sloe gin fizz in his eyes. I took to the woods.

I preach down at the campus, doze under the poncho, under the bridge, look out for the fists that shake or betray. There are fists that threaten an entire nation. I sing of this.

I speak to my children from out of the wilderness.

Happiness runs swiftly and so far ahead, and still, I think, we have the means to chase it.

Never forget that The Collection tells stories of joy and transformation, of self-definition and adaptation, of possibility, of hope growing from the holes in our greatest city.

I share the words of The Collection.

I don't weep for my loss.

The Collection begot the yard sale, and change is as inevitable as the nickels in your pocket.

In this paragraph the change is a semicolon; hereafter the words scramble themselves into meanings that break like eggs, shelled so delicately against the world. The Collection's a beautiful necessity these days. The Collection contains the plans for a City on a Hill. The Collection offers Hemingway's pipe and trousers, the novel that his wife lost (oh, the sentences are short, dry, straining for beauty out of the rough). The Collection holds Einstein's lost theorems. The Collection harbors the crumpled Bill of Rights. The Collection hands out Charlie Chaplin's jaunty little hat.

The Collection must be spoken of, remembered.

I gave it to my people. They put it to work.

FIVE STORIES ABOUT THROWING THINGS
AT FAMOUS PEOPLE

AUTHOR'S NOTE: *Although some of the names in this work might seem like clever anagrams, a closer inspection will reveal that they are not clever at all. Even if bored, celebrity-obsessed readers were to unscramble these anagrams into the names of certain public figures, the interactions between these unscrambled anagrams and my invented characters would remain an imaginary construct.*

I.

SOMETIMES THEY CALLED HIM by this nickname (I don't even like to think about it), like Sir February, except the title wasn't Sir and the month wasn't February, but you get the idea. This wasn't the only reason he seemed so haughty, but it was one of the reasons, as if they had given the month his name, rather than vice versa. Then those candy bars came out with his picture on them. They were called Jackie Bars!! (With two exclamation points. Two of them!!) And despite my misgivings, I couldn't deny that they were nougatly delicious. Three months later, I ended up with four cavities. (Two cavities per exclamation point!!)

Then his team came to town (and I hated that team, too, with its proud history of excessive pride and its pinstripes that looked like elegance if elegance were actually cheapness disguised as elegance), and I got a bleacher seat behind right field, where Jackie played. That day Jackie went four for five, and when he took the field for the bottom of the ninth, he tipped his hat to the bleachers. That was the point when I felt stabbed by hopelessness.

I did not want to kill Jackie Gregson; I wanted to give him four cavities and I wanted my month back, but I had a triple-A (Duracell) battery in my pocket and I figured I might as well throw it at him. So I reared back to throw, and I reared back some more (and as I had never reared before, it felt oddly exhilarating), and then I thought this wasn't such a good idea, and then I let loose, and something designed to be a single part of my shoulder ripped into two, and the battery plopped to the bright green turf approximately three and three-quarters yards to Jackie's left. He didn't seem to notice. (Since then I have had five shoulder operations, made thirty-five trips to the herbalist, been treated with magnets, crystals, needles, and weed. I've been divorced and fired and divorced and fired and fired and fired again. I've seen chiropractors and herpetologists and any other type of -ologist that sounds medicinal, even if it's not. Nothing works. So I have my reasons not to like Jackie Gregson.)

II.

Simple story really. Sort of sad. Sort of about America. Sort of about other things. Maybe other countries. Maybe Canada. Maybe not.

Me: laid off from the bank. Still wearing the suits Monday through Friday, dungarees on Saturday, chinos on Sunday. Kids grown, living on opposite coasts, lawyer on one, real estate agent on the other. Wife: working full time at the library. Me: playing pool five days a week, suit and tie, 50 cents a game down at the bar. Beating college kids—the girls, the boys, the in-betweens, the either-ors. College kids, jeans so tight they squeeze brains along with asses. Pabst Blue Ribbon: $1.25 a can.

System down perfectly. Leave in morning, after wife, play pool nine to four, $3.75 for beer, egg-salad sandwich in brown bag for lunch, dill pickle, oatmeal cookies, spit out raisins, 50 cents for first game of pool, challengers pay, winner plays on, play, play, play, play, get home, wife none the wiser. Me: winner.

System complicates: $7.50 for beer, $2 for pool.

System complicates: $10 for beer, $3.50 for pool.

System complicates: $13.75 for beer, $6 for pool, lunch lost by noon, tie missing by two.

System complicates: one night, night comes. Me: still at bar. Band playing in the corner, distracting.

Me: "Who they?"

Tight Pants: "Some band, The Fragments or something. From fucking Toronto."

Me: throwing can of Pabst Blue Ribbon in direction of stage, hitting wall to left of band. Me: regretful, still thirsty; can was three-quarters full. Just wanted to get band's attention, make request, maybe "Yes, We Have No Bananas," maybe "Edelweiss," something classy. Police: dislike my taste in music, making threats, jail or home. Tough decision.

Two days later. Me: manager at McDonald's. Tight-pantsed kids, smirk-faced, waiting for fried chunks of apple-ish pie.

III.

Try catching a live bat. Try it. Try it, and then come griping to me. Like I would go through that bullshit to have what happened happen. At the time it seemed like more than a good idea; it seemed in the neighborhood of great, perhaps even stupendorous, splendiferous, fantabulous. It seemed like one of those words that is so good it's impossible to spell.

Ruben Sozozoy, he liked his bats and stuff, meaning drugs. Ruben Sozozoy, he put on the best rock and roll show ever. Ruben Sozozoy, he was heavier than heavy, heavier than wearing a ten-pound sack of potatoes on your head. Ruben Sozozoy, he worshipped Satan, and he fired his guitar player every month, and he liked those smoke machines. Ruben Sozozoy, his shows were so great because he would bite the heads off bats and then shoot around the stage and pretend he was crazy, though it didn't always seem like he was pretending.

So I spent about all week, alone, staking out empty barns, climbing up in attics, staying very quiet on dark nights. It sounds exciting, but it was more like a long stretch of boring and then three seconds of pissed-off bat getting in your face. The day before the show, I caught one. I wore these thick old leather gloves, and the bat, all blackness and babyish drool, looked a little like my cousin Bobby. I named him Bobby the Bat, and I should have known right then that anything that looked that much like Bobby was going to be too sluggish for what I imagined.

When Ruben played one of those super-heavy songs, I would aim toward the stage and let loose. I figured Bobby would get into it. Bobby would fly toward Ruben, and then he would soar out of the stadium, and Ruben would point at Bobby, black and scary and powerful, like a soiled lung. Then Ruben would point at me, because I had created this moment, and then there would be many, many moments backstage with the girls and the halter tops spilled on the floor and the Tupperware bowls filled with cocaine and me talking about Bobby, the bat not the cousin.

To get into the show without a hassle, I wrapped Bobby up in Saran Wrap and then tinfoil, like a sandwich, and I slipped him into my back pocket. Twice, I sat on him by accident, and when I finally unwrapped him, he didn't seem batlike at all. I was in the pit in front of the stage, and Ruben was playing, and I just winged Bobby in front of me. Bobby never got into it. He just plopped onto the stage like he was totally bored with the whole flying idea. My bat was just lying there. Ruben kept playing and running around.

I yelled, "Come on, Bobby."

"Man," someone said, "it's Ruben up there. Cheer right."

Maybe three songs later, Ruben wandered over to Bobby. I could see him bend down, and I thought, This is it. Ruben opened wide and chomped down, and then he got this spacey look on his face. Then he ran off stage, and the show stopped like it crashed into a brick wall.

Later, years later, I found out that Ruben only bit fake bats, rubber ones, and that day, he ended up getting all those rabies shots, right in the sour pit of his stomach. Right then and there, though, I knew none of this. I was just scared. No one wanted that show to stop. No one was happy.

I started wondering if anybody saw me throw the bat, if anyone noticed. It was hard to say, but whether they knew or not, I could tell those people felt some kind of big, big hate; the stadium couldn't hold it. I could feel that hate roiling and burning, and it chased me all the way out to the parking lot and down the freeway and up the back road and into my living room, and it slept on my couch for days. Sometimes, when I look for lost and loose change, I can still feel that hate, smaller but stronger. It lurks between the cushions.

IV.

My lawyer has advised me not to say anything at all, especially about computers or monopolies or whatshisname, but you don't really throw the pie. You push it. That's the trick. Down with Gil Tables! Sorry. Please strike that from the record. You push the pie. That's all I'm saying.

V.

It was 30 years ago, when I was still in college, and I had the sort of bottom that attracted eyeballs and pinching fingers, and I was convinced that, if given the opportunity, Jose Mont's fingers and eyes would be drawn to my ass, like the waves to the shore. Every year that passes, I make my ass firmer and shapelier, until in my head it has become a luscious upside-down heart, something Rodin sculpted out of flesh and then became so enthralled with that he left the rest of me unsculpted. Even now, my breasts are flat and girly as if they had been pressed for years, like a dried corsage, between the heavy pages of a keepsake book. But this isn't about my breasts; if it were, they would be bigger. No, I had this ass and these ideas, so I drove out to Las Vegas, alone, free, young as spring, younger—I was so young I was still covered with an icy cool grace, grace like snow—and my plan was to get seduced by Jose Mont.

I had a hotel room and hot pants. I had pushed my way up to the front of the crowd. I had a pair of panties, worn the day before, stuffed in my shirt, and when I caught Jose Mont's eyes, the way everyone's eyes caught him, as if the crowd were a web of sex and hope, I threw my room key to the stage and the panties, and then I left.

Back at the hotel, I had to ask for another key. The man behind the counter had greasy gray curls, as if the top of his head were engulfed in storm clouds.

"All you fucking women with your extra keys," he said.

I wanted to say, "We certainly hope to be fucking women," but I thought he would miss the point or misconstrue it, and although I had spirit then, I did not yet have a thick tangle of guts to buoy me. The guy's fingers groped for the key, and he rolled over me with his slutty eyes.

I didn't say thank you. I didn't say anything. I went to my room. I took a long hot shower and climbed up on the bed without drying off. The water dripped off me into the comforter, and I felt like I was melting into the future. Then one of these things happened:

1. Jose Mont arrived. He cooed in my ear. We humped like humpback whales, and we didn't even know what that meant, but it sounded suitably leviathan. Eight months later I took a trip south of the border where I developed a fondness for tamales and I gave birth to our secret and subsequently adopted love child, Latino superstar Mark Trycini.

2. Jose Mont arrived. But the blood never arrived in his cigarillo-of-a-penis, and he just kissed my body for the entire night with professional rigor. His lips were chapped.

3. Jose Mont arrived. I won thirteen hundred dollars, a silk shirt, and one rhinestoned boot in eight and a half hours of high-stakes Gin Rummy. To this day, the boot swims in a sea of bric-a-brac out in my garage.

4. Jose Mont arrived. As I finished my last-minute precoital ablutions, he fell into a deep unshakable sleep on the vomit-brown carpeting. When I woke up the next morning alone in the bed, he was long gone. His only trace: a single rhinestoned boot.

5. Jose Mont arrived. He spent twelve minutes denting his shoulder against the bolted door I had reinforced with a dresser and a sixty-five-pound black-and-white TV. The police took him away with surprising discretion.

The story is a comfort to me. I own three Dunkin' Donuts franchises, have three nieces, two nephews, men to date, money to spend, freedom, glee, and a killer backhand. I play tennis like I am forty-two, but all that exercise only gives me a discount of eight years. The heart of my ass has become some other organ, still vital, less shapely, like a spleen, except in my memory.

A few years ago, I somehow ended up on this horrible blind date. This guy had this eerie way of lowering his voice, so it sounded like he was speaking in parentheses. He was still brushing the ashes of his last divorce off his sleeves, and I'll never forget his name—Larry October, like the month. All he wanted to talk about was throwing a battery at Jackie Gregson, the baseball player. Just by looking at Larry October, I could tell that this story had swallowed him up, and he lived in that story's stomach, and it would never spit him out. So Larry October told me his whole boring story, and when he came to the end, I said, "Tell it again in a different way."

"That's the story," he said. "I just told you."

So I told him the Jose Mont story, version no. 3, and then version 2, and then version no. 1.

"Jose Mont, Jose Mont, Jose Mont," he said. "What's the big deal about Jose Mont?"

"Jose Mont?" I said. "It's not about Jose Mont."

And it's true. Sometimes I don't think Jose Mont has to be in it at all.

EL AMERICANITO

WHEN HE FIRST DISCOVERED the strip bar at the end of the boiling avenue, Evan adopted a limp and spoke in a slow low tone, something he considered mature and raspy. He soon gave up his affectations. They didn't care how old he was. He had American dollars, and the girls patted his head, called him Americanito, called him muchacho. He ordered cerveza, and they brought him pineapple juice poured into Corona bottles. Once, when he was looking for the baño, he saw three of them topless, all three just standing there together, and they said, "Muchacho!" And he said, "Perdón," and they covered their nipples with their forearms. The girls were about nineteen, twenty, twenty-three, something collegey. He had just turned thirteen. He came once a week, on Friday afternoons, when his mother was buried in mud, in full spa mode. The club didn't really seem to be open. Acapulco's businessmen were napping through the tender burning part of the day, and Evan had the place to himself. Him and the girls.

Once an older stripper pressed her hand between his legs, and he felt his penis stiffen and spread out beneath her fingers. He enjoyed the stripper's hand on him and the way she pursed her lips into and then out of the word muchacho. She mentioned a sum in pesos. She had frizzy black hair and a crinkly smile. Something more could happen here. But Cristina came and brought him his drink, and she pulled the other stripper, the one with the hand, away. He heard them arguing.

Too fast for him to take it all in. He heard Cristina say, "niño . . . el niño."
Only Cristina came back to the table that afternoon.

Cristina usually sat down to talk, to work on her English he guessed.
She had a careful unaccented vocabulary. If you looked closely, her
cheeks displayed small painful marks, like the holes left by thumbtacks,
but her eyebrows were dancing tildes. He talked to her about America,
the different states, about schools and movies, sports and politics. She
had many, many questions.

"We call him Dubya," he said.

"And why do you call him this?" she asked.

It took him a while to explain.

Sometimes, when he used a large or strange word—he was particularly proud of *lugubrious*—he felt as if he had taught her something.
Sometimes her questions seemed unconnected and pointless. Sometimes they wrapped him up inside himself.

"Why do you play soccer?"

"I just do, that's all."

This didn't seem to satisfy her.

She sat next to him at the table, her eyes patient, brows restless, a
shawl-like thing covering parts of her he'd like to see, and he explained
the way the ball felt as it crinkled up your toes and up into your brain.

"When you kick it to where your teammate will be, not now but in a
second or two, that's what I like about it," he said.

"And how do you know this?" she asked.

"It's sort of a guess and a hope all mixed up," he said, and he let his
fingers become tiny bipeds, soccer players that acted it out for her on
the tabletop.

The strip club had seven round tables and a row of shady booths
and a small stage with a fireman's pole. Sometimes when Evan arrived, dresses were slopped onto the floor as if whoever had worn them
had suddenly and mysteriously dematerialized. The walls were cinder
blocks, the toilet a hole in the floor. There were no windows. Near the
baño, there were three small back rooms, cell-like and oddly furnished:
One held an unmade bed, the second a mattress spread on the floor,
the third a musty brown recliner. The entire place had a forced florality,
the kind of smell that suggested it covered up something much, much
worse.

Back at the hotel, he had his own suite, a microwave, a king-sized bed, a refrigerator, gold-flecked walls, mirrors on every surface, each reflecting his browned face, the swirl of blond in his chestnut hair where the beach sun had robbed the follicles of color. Every room in the building held a false chill, made him shiver himself into a sweatshirt.

At the hotel, he could order whatever he wanted for dinner, and then he would go down to his parents' suite, a bigger one, and eat his lump of protein while they pecked at their salads.

He said, "That would taste better with dressing."

His mother waved her fork as if she were shooing his words and calories out of the way.

Mexico had been parentally billed as an adventure, but mainly Evan lounged by the hotel pool, walked the beach, gorged himself with parasailing, discovered yesterday's seashells again today. When he wanted to play tennis, he blasted his serve over and over into a brick wall.

His mother had taught him tennis but no longer played. She was carefully blonded and dedicated to the eradication of hips and thighs. His father was tall and thick, and his manner walked a bridge suspended between jokey and calm; even his laughter was mellow, a chuckle that never revved beyond mirth. His mother had once said, "He's not like that in the boardroom," and Evan had stopped. He thought she said bedroom.

He said, "The where?"

For long desert stretches of afternoon, he and his mother had the entire hotel pool to themselves. One time he almost said, "The pineapple juice is better at the strip club," but he stopped himself after the word "better," and then he said, "than last time." She didn't seem to notice the delay. They shared spritzes of conversation.

He said, "Can I use the word bitch?"

She paused and said, "You may use it as a verb."

Then he splashed into the pool.

As their Mexican days frittered in the sun, his parents made plans. He had heard all the arguments for leaving him in Acapulco and all those for taking him to Cuba. Sometimes he wished they would talk about these things in another room.

His father said, "Should we get you some cigars?"

No one laughed. They had caught him smoking last year.

They would just be gone for the weekend, just Saturday and Sunday.

Just two days, and they left two weeks worth of people he could call on: everyone at the hotel, Leon at the pool, the Robersons, several men who worked with his father. They all had phone numbers and beepers. He had a list, a number for every emergency.

He had plans, too.

On Saturday night, he sauntered out of the hotel, down the avenue. The bouncer, Tito, the only man he had ever seen at the club, gave him a zippered-mouth look and then a thumbs-up.

Men were stuffed into the booths, and here and there women sat in various laps. Two strippers were naked and stretching on the stage, shimmying up the pole. Evan watched their legs and their buttocks. Their breasts flattened and then pillowed as they raised and lowered their arms. Techno music jolted through the club's bluish glow. Where did the blue come from? The women's bodies seemed infected with it, as if the color were a skin disease.

He looked at the women's hollowed places, smooth armpits, backs of knees, the clefts of their buttocks.

A number of fans whirred up in the ceiling, and they seemed to blow his thoughts around. He should leave. He should stay. He should find Cristina. He should find the woman who had grabbed him that time.

Someone, a man, said, "Hola, amigo," and he felt himself being pulled into a booth. Three men, all sullen and mustachioed, sat there.

One said, "Hello, little American."

Another said, "Quieres una cerveza?"

He drank beer with them, real beer this time, and he felt his thoughts get cool and soft-edged. He watched the women dance, and when the men whistled, he whistled, and when they clapped, he clapped. He bought beers for the three men and himself, he didn't recognize the waitress, and his dollars began to disappear.

He disliked the men, but he liked being there with them. They all wore shiny dull-colored suits and frowned at the women in an appraising way. The men ruined it. Would his father come here? No, there were only Mexicans. Evan was the only American, the youngest in the room. He slurped at the bitter cool tang of his beer.

He saw swatches of hair between the women's legs and scars and strips of muscle under their skin. He felt the heft of his penis pressing against the fly of his jeans.

He laughed with the men when his new fresh beer foamed up, and he tried to catch it all with one gulp, and his mouth felt wet yet dried-out and prickled by nettles. When he looked up, Cristina was there.

As she looked at him, her fingers laced her dress together, pulling shut the V designed to show off her bosom. Her face was paler, smoothed-over and flattened by makeup, and he saw all the curves of her underneath thin fabric, more of a film, a cloud, an idea, than an outfit.

She said, "Evan, you must go now," and she yanked him out of the booth, and she pulled him with her toward the back rooms. He heard the men laugh, and Cristina turned back, said, "Pendejos," and they laughed some more.

Evan could feel the skin of her hand and a strange hard bump on it. A wart? A callus? He imagined the two of them and the unmade bed, and then Cristina pulled him out a door and into an alley, the night, the heat, the dark, the lack of blue light, her gentle anger.

In her clear, proper English, she said, "You don't belong here now."

She wore high heels, stood taller than he, and the edge of her dress only dipped a few inches below her hips.

He said, "Tú eres bonita."

She looked at him carefully for several seconds. She didn't touch him. She looked some more, and then she tapped herself on the chest and said simply, "Usted."

His head snapped as if a wire holding it up had severed, and she seemed yet again taller, older, colder, foreign, questionless, unquestionable.

She said, "Necesitas dinero por un taxi?"

He shook his head, and she said, "Adiós."

The hotel was a few blocks, a half mile maybe away, but he wasn't used to the angles of night, and he found himself wandering in the wrong direction. He didn't have any money left, no taxi dinero. The darkness was hot, and the beach was dangerous when the sun went down: He knew that. He stayed on the avenue, where people looked at him but said nothing, nada.

As the sweat wrapped around him, he felt that his shirt was melting, and he remembered being caught out in a thunderstorm maybe two years before. The water had drained out of the sky, pelted the ground, pounded him. The thunder had exploded, and then the lightning sliced the sky. He wasn't supposed to be out in it, and when he got back home and he was drenched, his mother had put on her you-know-better-than-that-piss-moan-bitch voice. He looked up and expected to hear the crackle, see electricity flash and snarl. The actual night was cloudy and pitted but calm. There was no one to yell at him. This was his big night, and the sky had nothing to say.

In the morning, he woke up with a mewling belly and a graveled head. He vomited several times and dunked his face in the sink. He nearly cried, then dialed the front desk, asked Julio to bring him some Alka-Seltzer. Did anyone see him come in so late, all drunk and sweaty, all vagranty? He guessed so but couldn't fish out any memories of the night before beyond the heat and the storm he had made up in his head. Then thoughts of the strip club spilled all over him.

He found solace in bottled water and artificial sixty-two-degree sleep. He buried the rest of the weekend under blankets and sheets, muffled his head with pillows.

Back from Cuba, his parents arrived bearing gifts and bags beneath their eyes.

"Wretched place," his father said.

His mother said, "The worst hotel I've ever seen."

Evan said, "I got sick and puked everywhere."

His mother pushed his hair back from his eyes and said, "You're better now."

It wasn't a question. Their hotel informants, he figured, had very likely informed.

During his last week in Mexico, he loitered in the vicinity of the strip club. He had his own gravity, he thought. He would orbit the place, simply revolve, never arrive. He saw women who looked like Cristina, but this resemblance required corners of eyes and squinting. When Friday came, he prided himself on his sure and perfect absence from the club.

Two days before Evan left the country, a family of Mexicans accosted him. Four little boys, two shirtless, none of whom came up higher than his armpits. A mother, a father, both much younger than his parents. Their clothes, something like soccer outfits, were shiny polyester, bright colors: neon green, a leering red. Tourists, he thought, too poor to come except during the off season.

They were standing near a church, and the father said to him, "Tomas una fotografía?"

Evan stared for a second, a dollop of near-thought. He was about to tap himself on the chest, say firmly, "Usted." Instead he held his arms out like dilapidated wings, said, "I don't speak Spanish."

The boys mimed taking photos. Four tiny imaginary cameras. The boys were skinny and sun-roasted. The mother, brusque and sure and long-haired, pressed a scratched plastic camera into his hands.

The family shifted and giggled, showing off a surplus of teeth and poses, and the father encircled them all with his arms. The mother laughed.

He snapped the picture of them, and then they pelted him with more Spanish, and he had to pretend it glanced off him, their words just chunks of nonsense, spittle, hail. The littlest pulled on his arm. They wanted him to join the picture.

They lined the boys up from smallest to biggest, and Evan was placed between the oldest son and the father. The boy next to him wrapped his arm around his waist; the father draped his hand over Evan's shoulder. The mother manned the camera. The boy looked at him and laughed and smiled. The father smelled of cigarettes and some strong clingy soap.

The sun made a hot bitter face at him. Finally he smiled with them, couldn't help it. He also laughed, and then the family waved their adióses.

Two days later, he was on his way back to the States. His parents sat one row ahead of him. Evan had his own leathery aisle in first class.

Evan ordered a beer from the stewardess, and his father poked his silvered head into the aisle, twisted it around so he faced Evan and the stewardess.

"You leave *that* down in Mexico. He'll have a ginger ale."

The stewardess said, "Sorry."

Evan swirled his ginger ale around the clarity of ice. The movie wouldn't start for a half hour. The GameBoy was up in the overhead compartment, not worth the effort.

At Choate, he decided, he would study French; all the Spanish had been scooped out of him. The soda fizzed and swished.

Now, far above the surf and the cinder blocks, he felt like he could have his way with her. He would strip her down.

But questions covered Cristina's breasts: "In America do you live in a big house?" "What do you study in school?" And her loins: "What does

George Bush think about Mexico?" Even her feet: "Why do you wear those fat red sneakers?"

Each question was a veil covering her. But when she pulled off "How do you play tennis?" she would be covered by "And what state do you live in?" She would never strip herself fully this way, and he didn't care. This was confusing, a pebble troubling the tread of his mind.

He pictured the family instead. The mother pulling the photos out of the envelope. The children pushing out their fingers at one shot in particular. He imagined their shock and surprise, their wonder, when they looked at the empty spot in the picture where Evan should have been. The American had simply disappeared from their photograph.

And that is where Evan would have liked the scene to stop.

Instead the imaginary father looked at the photo, shook his head wisely, said something cruel and unexpected and true.

"Remember we didn't take this photo for us," he said softly. "He was rich and American, but he reeked of loneliness."

BIG SPRINGS

Ronnie didn't always look this way, cropped blond hair like a boy's and stubbed fingernails. She scrapes the plaque off your teeth, and you spit when she says, "Go ahead." You fear her comments about flossing and her tone as she reshapes your misconceptions about gum disease. Years ago, you wouldn't have imagined letting her fingers into your mouth.

Years ago is when I met her.

Years ago, she was lying there completely stripped. Her hair was matted and trampled and fluffy in other parts, and we both smelled of cigarettes, and the spirit of alcohol clung to us, and our bodies fit like two seeds wedged together into the earth. You would think two people could just relax and enjoy this, and at first it seemed as if we would just stew in this moment. Ronnie began to sing, and it was a slow, grizzled song, something people sing in church. It was a new kind of peaceful for me, and I even dozed off. When I woke up, she was still singing this same song. I let my fingers brush up her thighs. This is when she started to tell me about all those brothers and her dead baby and her dead old mother.

Her youngest brother, older than her by five years, picked at the scab of his life. When he was seventeen years old, he stole a television set and was shot through the back three careful times. Her oldest brother was promoted to second lieutenant shortly before the accident. His jeep skittered off a wintery road, and his body wasn't found for several days. Even when he was a teenager, her middle brother had a belligerent puffy face, and he carried the weight of whiskey on his bones. He now serves his time at the U.S. Penitentiary in Leavenworth. When Ronnie was eighteen, she lost a baby. And her mother has been dead since Ronnie was fifteen. Cancer. It picks its victims with few if any prejudices.

All of these people died literally or symbolically in a place called Big Springs, Nebraska. Ronnie can rattle them off. She speaks of them all as if they were recently buried, even the brother in Leavenworth. She's got a dead worry for each finger of the hand she makes into a fist.

She punched that fist into me before we even said hello.

We met in Lincoln. In a bar known for not much of anything. It had pink walls, and it served strong drinks. Maybe I wouldn't have even talked to her in another room. It was the kind of place where people press up and surround the bar. You need to skirmish and holler just to get served. I sort of pushed this gal, pretty but all gunked up with makeup. I didn't say sorry. I didn't say anything.

She hit me four sharp times right in the biceps. Her knuckles were searching for a bruise.

And I said, "What the fuck."

And she said, "I'll have a gin and tonic, darling."

She had hair like a haystack. It was engineered with all kinds of sprays, and her jeans bit into her curves and her angles. A few hours later, when I slipped my hand down her back and onto her ass, she looked up at my face, and her mouth was a pinch of flesh. It could have been good, or it could have been bad.

We went back to the place I was staying.

I took off her denim jacket, her T-shirt, her black bra, and then I watched her spread out on the carpet and strip off her jeans. She had to struggle and kick at them, and when they were finally off, red creases marked where the denim had clenched her.

We didn't so much make love as jury-rig it. Staple it together. Spit on it and add friction. She pinched and rubbed and splayed out across the bed and offered and demanded.

She said, "Not yet, not yet, not yet."

The whole night was about motion and waiting.

The next morning, as my hands skimmed over the naked shape of her, she told me about her brothers, her mother, and even the baby, dead and buried and bearing the genes of a man she now hates.

I would have preferred she didn't mention any of these people.

We had flesh and a clear Sunday of nothing needing to be done, and it seemed like these things could just find another place in her mind. I said this very thing to her.

She said, "You asshole, you fucker, you shithead, you fuckface."

All of this was in a mellow tannish voice, and it reminded me of an old pair of boots I used to wear. I was able to stomp my way through all of these words.

She said, "You're gonna say sorry."

She did not punch me again, although she made menacing motions. She stood up on the mattress. She bounced several times. She collapsed on top of me.

Her voice turned slushy: "You'll submit. I don't care what you say."

She offered up her brown little nipples. She pulled on my hair.

"You can nip, but don't bite. You bite, and I'll pull those teeth."

She poked her fingers into me. She twisted my head. She messed my story up with hers.

To tell Ronnie's story, you have to go all the way back to Big Springs, near the Colorado border. She grew up there. It's the kind of place people like you think of and say "uh-yup," and "hicks" and "Where the men are men, and the sheep are scared." If you've been there, you don't know it. You just got in the car and watched the needle drift back to F, and Big Springs wilted away in the rearview mirror.

Big Springs, Ronnie explained, was not exactly hard. Instead it was more like a constant kind/cruel scratch down your spine. And when she said this to me, she ran her own sharpened fingernail down my arm. It didn't tickle, although her voice bubbled up, squeaked, teased even.

We drove down I-80, took Exit 107, drifted into town.

As far as I can tell Big Springs has nine streets and five hundred people, but this number is dying. Folks grow old and frozen, and they expire, or they just get up and leave. Those that stay have the fields and the coffee shop (opening, closing, opening again) and the pool hall and the Char Bar and the Bosselman truck stop and the wheat in the ground and the bills to pay. The grain elevator's the only object fighting against gravity, and it's a dirty bone-white. Ronnie's dad worked there for a time, and he fell from a great height and busted several ribs and both legs. This does not count in Ronnie's list of tragedies, minor or major.

In winter, the entire world has a crust of gray meanness. It's not a place for people who can't find ways to live in their own heads.

Summer's better, full of work and flat sprints of green and growth and all the water coming up out of the earth and then joining it again.

We went back there, and I helped her father walk down long rows of corn. We opened up little gates in a pipe and let water sweep out into the crops. He has a crooked way of walking, and his eyes are fading into the gray of his hair.

We drank warm beer that curdled on our tongues. The water was cool, and it gurgled into the green and the dirt, and the mud tried to swallow up our boots. We slurped at our beers, and the world licked us with its blue sun-stained tongue.

All those rows made me think of your tract house and all its relations. All those homes planted in the ground, in tight hard rows, to the west of Omaha. There's no space between them. Nothing to see except your neighbor's house and me pulling up in the Roto-Rooter truck.

I have refitted your toilets and unclogged your sewage, and I see the lack of dirt on your carpet and also the shit you flush away, bury deep beneath the land. People like you have a way of hiding nothing.

After I bless your burnt-out pipes and wash my hands and write out the bill, I am going to drive home slowly. I may tell Ronnie about you. I may tell her about the mole on your forehead. I may tell her about the sexy paperback wedged between your toilet tank and the wall. I may just whistle and forget all about you. We live way out past your tract house and past the tract houses after that.

I am not one who fixates on the origins of things. There's a beginning, sure, and if you wait long enough, it's a memory, a spot in the rearview.

I have been to Big Springs many, many times now. It's not the kind of place you know. Watch for it on the highway. There's a whole great feeling of life there that you wouldn't quite be able to tally up. There's a woman, ninety-two years or something, and entire works of Shakespeare live inside her head. Ronnie has spoken to me in this woman's voice, whistled a whisper of a scream, saying, "Out, out, damn spot." This old woman has lived her entire life surrounded by the nothing of Big Springs. Ronnie told me about her, but she's not the kind of person you'd know. Know or imagine.

ACKNOWLEDGMENTS

Even if these thanks stretched for miles, I'm still afraid I would leave out someone who belongs in.

I would not be writing stories at all if it weren't for the guidance and support of three excellent writers and mentors: Tom Lorenz at the University of Kansas, Trudy Lewis at the University of Missouri, and John Vernon at Binghamton University. They told me what I needed to hear when I needed to hear it—and, no, it wasn't always good news.

Eleven stories in this collection appeared previously, sometimes in slightly altered form. With one exception (thanks again, Tom), those stories came out of the slush pile, and I am grateful to the editors who took a chance on my work: Elaine Bartlett, Jody Brooks, Danit Brown, Chris Bundy, Christine Butterworth-McDermott, Mary Carroll-Hackett, Meg Galipault, Paul Ketzle, David Lynn, Jason Rizos, Mike Rutherglen, Jonna Semeiks, Anna Christina Shearer, Mary Troy, and Martin Tucker. The stories appeared in the following literary magazines: "The Collection" (as "The Immaculate Collection") in *Confrontation*; "This Document Should Be Retained as Evidence of Your Journey" in *Cottonwood*; "El Americanito" in *Dos Passos Review*; "The Chez du Pancakes" in *Indiana Review*; "Amar" in *Kenyon Review*; "Maria" and "Big Springs" in *Meridian*; "Five Stories about Throwing Things at Famous People" in *Natural Bridge*; "The Dirty Boy" in *New South*; "Boy, Sea, Boy" in *Quarterly West*; and "The Kids" in *REAL: Regarding Arts and Letters*.

I'd also like to thank Chris Chambers, Jeff Chan, Kenneth E. Harrison

Jr., Carrie Jerrell, Martin Lammon, Jill Patterson, Eamonn Wall, Amy Sage Webb, and Kellie Wells for supporting and publishing my fiction. Over the years, many other readers and editors have sent me words of encouragement. The gatekeepers of the "little magazines" help maintain the soul of the literary world, and I hope all writers are thankful for what they do.

This book grew up in Lawrence, Kansas, and in Berea, Ohio. I am truly grateful for the four years of generous support provided by the Madison and Lila Self Graduate Fellowship at the University of Kansas. Moreover, numerous professors at KU offered me the gift of their smarts and their time. In particular, I'd like to thank Philip Barnard, David Bergeron, Byron Caminero-Santangelo, Maxine Clair, Katie Conrad, Carolyn Doty, Dorice Elliott, Iris Smith Fischer, Doreen Fowler, Carolyn Jewers, Mike Johnson, Beth Manolescu, and Robin Rowland. Many of my KU friends have read some of these stories and commented on them, shared classrooms with me, or simply hung out while "talking books"—often a euphemism for "drinking beer." Iain Ellis, Kirby Fields, Loyal Miles, Cliff Phillips, Adam Powell, Mark Scoggins, Emily Stamey, Mike Stigman, Shawn Thomson, and Mary Wharff deserve special note—next round's on me.

In Berea, I am thankful for the support of my wily Greek adviser, Ted Harakas, and many other colleagues and friends. Erik Bailey, Mike Dolzani, Ron Ehresman, Mary Lou Higgerson, Sharon Kubasak, Karen Long, Terry Martin, Andy Mickley, Mike Riley, Margaret Stiner, and Marc Vincent have been particularly generous with their insights, their good cheer, or, in the case of Marc, their genius for practical jokes.

In my deep dark past at the University of Missouri, I made smart, funny friends like Mike Land, Bart Wacek, and Peter Weed, and I was pushed as a writer and a thinker by Sue Crowley, Indira Ganesan, Karl Grubaugh, Doug Hunt, Peter St. Onge, and Dave Sharp.

I am grateful to everyone affiliated with the University of Massachusetts Press—particularly Carol Betsch, Noy Holland, Sally Nichols, Carla Potts, Bruce Wilcox, and Leni Zumas—for their time, their enthusiasm, and their faith in this book.

Some of these stories were written in the third-floor apartment in the Hanson-Ballard house on Tennessee Street in Lawrence, Kansas. I can think of few better places to write (Paris? Madrid?) in this world. The Ballards and Hansons and Hanson-Ballards let me tramp through their home and offered their kindness and their washing machine and their wagging tails (in the cases of Bear, Kingsley, and Freddy, whom I mostly forgive for his early morning barking).

In Berea, I am supported by Winks, when he isn't biting, and Paco, the many-named cat. I'm grateful for my students at Baldwin-Wallace College, the happy people at the post office, and the Book & Bean.

My parents, Alfred G. Hoyt Jr. and Shirley Kinnie Hoyt, and my sister, Karen Hoyt Frankel, have put up with me and encouraged me all my life. They deserve several acknowledgment pages unto themselves.

I'd like to thank coffee and, also, red wine. I'd like to thank The Replay Lounge, The Bottleneck, The Tap Room, and Harbour Lights. I'd like to thank the dearly departed Paradise Cafe. I'd like to thank Charles Dickens, Denis Johnson, Guided by Voices, Voided by Guises, Slint for "Good Morning, Captain" (and Sasha Frere-Jones for his comment about it), Raymond Carver, The Hardaways, Sleater-Kinney, Steve Earle, and "Let There Be Rock" by the Drive-By Truckers.

I'd like to thank whoever's still reading this right now.

And most of all, I'd like to thank Sarah, who helps me figure out life's puzzles, and I'm not just talking about Sunday when the *Times* arrives.